LAURIE MANTELL
Murder and Chips

WALKER AND COMPANY · NEW YORK

All the characters and events portrayed in this story are
fictitious.

First published in the United States of America in 1982 by the
Walker Publishing Company, Inc.

This paperback edition first published in 1984.

ISBN: 0-8027-3072-8

Library of Congress Catalog Card Number: 81-71202

Printed in the United States of America

10 9 8 7 6 5 4 3 2 1

CHAPTER I

DETECTIVE SERGEANT Steven Arrow was a long way from home. Home was Lower Hutt where he was assistant to Detective Chief Inspector Jonas Peacock, head of the local Criminal Investigation Branch. This morning Steven had travelled the twelve miles around the edge of the harbour to Wellington airport, taken an early plane across Cook Strait to Nelson, a city in the north-west corner of the South Island.

Now he sat in the Number Two Court of the modern courthouse, a bright airy room, blonded-wood fittings, brown and gold carpet. Two narrow tables filled the central portion of the floor, the first occupied by three men, civilians, one large and beefy with close-curled grey hair, the others thinner, parchment-dry, aloof.

Immediately behind them was a group of Nelson police, the investigating team plus a quiet withdrawn man, bald, pince-nez, the local pathologist.

At a small table aslant by the witness box, a man and a woman were conversing in low tones, notebooks in front of them. Reporters, probably, from the local papers.

Steven shared the first row of the public sector with five other witnesses summoned, as he had been, to attend the court at the coroner's pleasure. Behind him, Steven could hear subdued whisperings from a surprising number of curious Nelsonians.

Usually, inquiries into an unexpected death were ignored by the public, only principals attending, such as coroner, police, people directly involved—and the press. Nelson, however, seemed particularly interested in the death of Cody Te Whenua Pyke—the man who had been discovered smothered in the chip pile.

The chip pile! That *had* to be the reason for this unexpected interest. Anyone living in Nelson was intensely aware of the chip pile.

Sawmills to the west chewed up southern beech, radiata pine, into small flat chips around an inch square. This product was transported in fleets of trucks to Port Nelson, piled into small hillocks to await shipment. When the Japanese ships arrived anything up to 18,000 tons would be loaded pneumatically, great funnels throwing chips into the ships' holds at the force of a high-velocity wind.

The constantly-renewed chip pile covered an unfenced area of over two acres, massily-packed up to thirty feet high, white pine chips on the left, red beech chips on the right, hopper and loading mechanism in between.

The body of Cody Pyke had been found close to the hopper buried under a fall of beech chips. An unusual death. An intriguing death—with so many odd factors.

A slight stir announced the arrival of the coroner. He walked into the room followed by his secretary and a man carrying an electric typewriter. The typewriter was set on the blonded table below the bench, plugged in, and the man left. The stenographer sat down, the coroner took his place, faced his audience. The court of Coroner Harrison T. Sturt was in session.

Steven listened absently to the opening proclamation being intoned by one of the local uniform men, glanced briefly at the press table.

Both reporters were busily writing, probably recapitulating known facts to make their copy more interesting for readers. Yet, if the coroner placed a stay on proceedings—if police declared investigations were still under way, nothing could be published. Nothing! The inquest would be used to establish identity, then adjourned to an unspecified date after completion of any and all criminal proceedings.

Somehow Steven did not think that was going to happen. Already press releases quoted "There were no suspicious circumstances," and "At this point in time the police were not looking for anyone else in respect to this death." All the journalese that meant nothing. Words that could be easily retracted if anything sensational occurred at the inquest. Obviously the press hoped so. Obviously the spectators hoped so.

Steven's own instincts told him the finding would be "accident" or some such. Except that he had been called. Why? He could add little to the statement he had already made to the investigating team. Therefore the summons meant Sturt himself was not satisfied, was anxious that Steven's information be placed on public record— public being somewhere out of police files.

It was unlikely Sturt was interested in the victim. Oddly enough, Cody Pyke came from Steven's own police district. He had lived in Petone, a borough on the northern shore of Wellington harbour,

6

south of and bordering on Lower Hutt itself. His father owned a small business, was a voluntary social worker, friend and counsellor to wayward youth.

Now Cody was dead. In Nelson. No one knew why he had come to Nelson. When found, the body had been clothed in semi-Spanish style—narrow black trousers, bright yellow shirt, scarlet matador jacket with a wide cummerbund of blue.

The fact that the outfit was a perfect facsimile of the uniform worn by male staff on cabaret nights at Nelson's five star hotel, the Rutherford, had aroused suspicions. Police had done an inconclusive feasibility study around the possibility that Cody was trying to infiltrate in order to commit some felony at the hotel.

It was possible. On cabaret nights casual staff were employed. Most were students earning extra money to help them through their year of study. On Saturday night, sixteen casuals had been engaged, only a few well-known to permanent hotel staff. Even the casuals, supplied by a reputable agency, were not necessarily acquainted with each other. The ten males were issued with matador uniforms from the hotel store, the six females given red-skirted gypsy costumes.

It was established that a male dressed right, behaving correctly, would not be challenged, no matter on which floor he was seen. He could be on room service call, delivering meals, drinks, running other errands. He could also of course be "ripping-off" the guests, slipping into their rooms and robbing them while they were occupied downstairs with the entertainment. All speculation. Nothing proven.

The local man finished speaking. The coroner shuffled papers in front of him, glanced briefly at the public benches. In hard rasping tones, he outlined the finding of the body of Cody Te Whenua Pyke in the chip pile at Port Nelson, began to call witnesses.

The first one was the beefy man with tight grey curls. He stood there showing a face meant for smiling, sagging now into folds of sadness. Thick-voiced, mumbling, he gave his evidence, brown eyes downcast to hands clenched in front of him.

Yes, he had viewed the body. Yes, it was his son, Cody Te Whenua Pyke. No, he did not know his son was in Nelson. Not until the police had called on Wednesday. At first he did not believe the body could be his son. He was sure Cody was at Hastings. The police insisted he contact Cody's friends. They told him they did not know where he had gone. They had all planned to go to Hastings that weekend but Cody had pulled out at the last moment. No, he

7

did not know why his son was wearing the clothes he was shown. He had never seen them before. Yes, his son did drink heavily at times—a matter of great sadness to his parents. But he was not drunk this time. Only a few drinks, the pathologist said. No, he could not understand why his son went to the chip pile. He could not understand why his son came to Nelson at all.

His son did not talk to his parents much—considered them old-fashioned, clinging to the old ways. His son preferred the new ways, cars, motorbikes, noisy music. Yes, Cody often went away for days on end. Sometimes he would tell them where he was going. Sometimes he would not. They did not press him, not wishing to alienate him. This time he had told them he was going to Hastings with his friends. They had accepted that.

His son was a good boy—but weak, easily led. There was no truth in the things people were saying—about why he was wearing those particular clothes. No truth. His son was dead. Why were the police trying to blacken his name? Trying to make him look like a criminal. The police were wrong. His son would not do anything like that. He wouldn't—

The big man stopped, hands over his face to hide his shame. Hurriedly the coroner excused him, watched sympathetically as the stricken man was led back to his seat by one of the men Steven had identified as legal representatives.

When everyone was settled again, Sturt lifted a piece of paper from the pile in front of him. It was, he explained, the pathologist's report which showed the deceased had died of suffocation. Ordinarily, a finding of accidental death would follow automatically but there had been so much speculation, so many unfounded rumours circulating about this particular death that it was felt all the known facts should be made public. He called to the stand the finder of the body, one Basil Horatio Atwill. A slight nervous man with sunken cheeks, overbright eyes, leaped to his feet, made his way to the stand.

Yes, his name was Basil Horatio Atwill. He was employed by Nelson Pine Forest Limited. His job was driving a bulldozer at the pile, keeping the chips packed down to a uniform level. He came to work on the morning of 5th February. First thing he noticed was the beech chips had spilled. A bad spill. It filled the area usually kept clear by the hopper. He decided it would be easier to use a shovel to clear the chips away from the machinery first. That's when he found the body. He yelled for the foreman and together they shifted enough chips to get the body out. Yeh, they guessed the joker was dead straight away. The foreman told him to keep everyone away so he stayed there while the foreman went to ring the police.

The foreman was called to corroborate this evidence. Questioned about security, he said standard security only was maintained, aimed at the prevention of vandalism and possible arson. No, there was little vandalism although people roamed around all the time. The area was well-roaded, with warehouses and transport storage depots all around. A marina adjacent to the wharf held a large number of pleasure craft—so no one would take too much notice of a stray car, even a pedestrian, no matter how late at night. Yes, people did fish off the wharf but apparently no one had done so that Saturday night. No, he had no idea why the man was at the chip pile. Could be any reason. Shelter? Warmth? A cool breeze blowing off the sea that night. Could have been looking for a place for a quiet drinking session.

Well, a couple of bottles there—full—and he smelled like a wino. Maybe he dug out a hollow not realising he would bring the whole lot down on top of himself.

Police Sergeant Ralston described the steps taken to seal off the area till the scene squad arrived. He noticed the clothes of deceased were similar to those worn by staff at the Rutherford so he interviewed the manager. The manager agreed to view the body but did not recognise him. At the same time the manager mentioned an incident that had happened on Saturday night, witnessed by a guest at the hotel, Detective Sergeant Steven Arrow of the Lower Hutt Police District.

"Yes, yes," said Sturt peevishly. "We'll get to that later. What other steps did you take to identify the body?"

"Usual procedural inquiries, sir. A description and artist's sketch in the local paper. Fingerprints to Head Office. On Tuesday the manageress of Cumberland House phoned to say the sketch looked like a guest who had gone out Saturday, had not returned. Acting on this advice we identified the deceased as Cody Te Whenua Pyke, resident of Petone. We notified Petone police and they contacted the lad's parents."

Steven was watching Pyke Senior during all this testimony, watched him wince every time the word "deceased" was used.

Now the body had been named. It had assumed an identity of its own and still no one knew why Cody Pyke had come to Nelson.

The manager of the Rutherford was called.

He definitely established the clothing of the deceased had never

9

been issued by the hotel. He pointed out minor differences, particularly quality of the material, lack of maker's tags. The court was left in no doubt that the clothing was a fairly successful copy of standard issue to hotel employees.

The coroner looked at the clock. "Well," he said slowly, "we have reached a suitable stopping place so we shall adjourn until two-thirty."

He stood up and everyone followed his example, leaving the courtroom. As Steven joined the crowd going down the wide stairway, he picked out a familiar face.

Inspector Brian Fairbrother, uniform branch, grinned up at him, moved over to wait by the bottom step. Until recently, Fairbrother had been Senior Sergeant in charge of Petone station. When promoted to Inspector, he transferred to the Nelson Police District and Steven had not seen him since the time Steven's superior, Detective Chief Inspector Jonas Peacock, had investigated the Blaney case, a little over three years ago.

The two men shook hands, Fairbrother saying, "Heard you were going to be here. What about a spot of lunch together? Then you can bring me up to date on what's been happening up your way."

He steered Steven along the street to a nearby vintage-type hotel, two-storey, wooden, cream and brown, galvanised roof—"a bit old fashioned but sets a decent table"—all the time exchanging news of mutual acquaintances.

They had a reunion drink together before moving into the dining-room, with its snowy tablecloths contrasting sharply with the dark red carpet, dark panelled walls. Steven selected steak Hawaiian from the menu, settled back to listen to Fairbrother.

The inspector opened blandly enough. "What did Jonas think about your being summoned to the inquest?"

"Didn't think it was necessary. Neither did I. You had my statement. Could've used that, couldn't you?"

"Could've. But Sturt wanted you down here. You. In person."

"What d'you think he's up to? Sturt, I mean."

"Hard to say. Got something on his mind, I guess. Tell that by the way he's conducting the inquest. Going into all those little bits and pieces. Haven't you noticed?"

"Some. One or two things he let slip by though. For instance, body discovered Monday morning. Rutherford's manager told you of my little episode. You contacted me Monday afternoon. Body still not identified. Tuesday this manageress rang and from that you established identity. Tuesday. Yet you didn't notify the parents until Wednesday."

Fairbrother smiled thinly. "Hope nobody else noticed that. But, y'see, it wasn't quite as smooth sailing as Ralston implied. The person missing from the Cumberland, well, last seen Saturday night wearing dark trousers, white shirt, blue jacket. Around eightish. His name was not Pyke. Not according to the register. Not according to the copies of flight tickets we found in a drawer of his room."

He nodded solemnly at Steven's show of surprise.

"I'm afraid we were sidetracked for a while—trying to locate the person listed on the register—or a relative thereof. As soon as we realised we were on a false trail we gave the room a thorough going-over, found some scraps of paper in the pocket of an overnight bag. We wondered about them. I mean, torn up yet kept, if you know what I mean. So we did a bit of jigsaw—made them into an envelope addressed to Cody Pyke, Petone."

"I see. They showed the name to you, being so recently from Petone—and you recognised it."

"Did I ever! Asa Pyke, the father—he's tops. One of the best. Helped us time and time again with young offenders. Straightened out quite a few potentials. Never ever heard of any of his own getting into trouble."

"So, as far as you're concerned, young Cody's clean?"

"He's clean. Doesn't prove he hasn't been playing around though. Just proves he's never been caught. Or maybe first time out. Kicking over the traces out of dad's bailiwick. Happens."

It happened. The parson's son. The policeman's son. The social worker's son. The father too busy with the problems of other people's children to have enough time for his own. It happened.

"What plane are you taking out?" asked Fairbrother.

"The five-thirty. If this damn inquest ever gets finished. Thought it would be over and done with this morning. Had other plans for this afternoon but now—" He sighed, looked around. "D'you think they'd mind if I used the phone?"

"No, go ahead. Ask them. But maybe it's something I can do for you. Be glad to help out."

Steven looked at him speculatively. "Nothing much. But last weekend—when Kylie and I were down here—we went out to one of these pottery places. Edenware they call it."

"Every valley hereabouts has its own little group of potters. But Edenware—that's way out past the marble quarries, isn't it?"

"That's right. We bought a coffee set for the bride. That's why we were down here. Kylie's cousin's getting married and she told us she'd love an Edenware coffee set. We had a good browse around while we were out there—some marvellous stuff! One thing Kylie—and I—fell in love with. Sort of bowl, labelled 'Petal'. Shaped like a large magnolia petal, y'know, roundish with the top edge wavy. Really attractive but also pricey. We let it go. Now, we're kicking ourselves because we didn't get it while we had the chance."

Fairbrother chuckled in sympathy. "So you want me to go out to Edenware and pick up this Petal bowl for you?"

Steven laughed. "No. No. It could be gone. Look, I'd like to ring. If it's still there maybe I could jack something up."

They left the dining room to locate the telephone. Steven looked up Edenware, dialled the number, waited. And waited. There was no answer. The distant ringing kept on and on and on.

He rejoined Fairbrother in the lounge. Fairbrother smiled. "No sweat. Try again. Plenty of time."

Steven tried the number again without success, then it was time to return to the courthouse.

Steven was called almost immediately to the stand. He identified himself, waited quietly for the coroner to start his questioning.

"You were at the Rutherford on the night of 3rd February?"

"Yes, sir."

"Will you please recount the incident you witnessed that night."

"On the night of 3rd February at exactly 9.35 I was looking out of the window of a suite on the seventh floor—"

"Your suite?"

"No, sir. The suite of a friend." He paused. "I was not resident at the hotel, merely visiting. As I said, I was looking out of the window when I noticed trouble in the car park. Three men, one dressed as an hotel employee. They seemed to be arguing. The man dressed in employee's clothing kept shaking his head, pointing towards the hotel. The others seemed to be urging him to get into a black car parked nearby. He wouldn't go. Another man got out of the car, walked over to the group. He came up behind the employee, lifted his hands to the man's shoulders and, at the same time, the other two grabbed the fellow's hands. He began to struggle—"

"And you just watched?"

"Until that moment, sir. As soon as I realised what was going on, I rushed to the phone, called the desk, saying one of their men was being attacked in the car park. I heard the girl call out to someone so I went back to the window in time to see the car door closing. Some men came running around the corner of the hotel towards the car park but by then the car was going out the far exit."

"What kind of car?"

"A black Holden station wagon. I couldn't see the number."

"That wasn't the end of the episode?"

"No, sir. The manager came up to see me later. Questioned me fairly closely about it. Seems they took a head count of all the staff and no one was missing."

"So he did not believe you had seen what you said you had?"

"He believed me. Said the hotel uniform suggested a gang planning to rip off the hotel guests. Maybe they were arguing about whether the pickings would be good enough."

"And you? Did you agree?"

"Well, it was a possibility."

Sturt shuffled his papers, looked sideways at Steven, sideways at the men at the first table. "Mr Walmsford is acting for Mr Asa Pyke. I understand he wishes to question you in this matter." He gestured towards the taller of the two men with the big man at the first table. "Mr Walmsford?"

Walmsford nodded, stood up, moved to the front of the table.

"Sergeant, I understand the night was overcast so the dark came early. Yet you claim you could see what happened clearly."

"Reasonably clearly. They were close to one of the lamps on the west side of the car park."

"But you cannot tell us the number of the car?"

"I was on the seventh floor. Looking down on the car park."

"Could you identify any of these men?"

"No. The same thing applies. Besides—two were wearing hats."

"So you cannot swear that the man wearing the hotel uniform was the same man whose body was found in the chip pile?"

"No."

"You will concede there could be another reason why young Pyke was also dressed in this outfit?"

"Yes."

"In other words, you cannot in truth claim that Cody Pyke was anywhere near the hotel at the time you said he was."

"I did not say he was at the hotel," Steven said patiently.

"But you did imply he was."

"I said that someone dressed in hotel employee clothing was there. That he had been attacked. That's all."

13

"Then how was it that the police started this ugly rumour that young Pyke was planning to—er—rip off the guests?"

Steven stiffened. "I doubt police started any such rumour. Other people knew about the circumstances."

"But the police did pursue inquiries along those lines?"

"Naturally. It was too much of a coincidence—"

"But you admit that was all it was, Sergeant. A coincidence. The police were unable to establish any connection."

"That is correct."

"You do agree, then, that Cody Pyke is quite innocent of any felonious intent despite the sinister interpretation the police have placed on this—coincidence?"

"There was no sinister interpretation—"

"Come now, Sergeant. You have to admit some ugly rumours have been circulating. Rumours that are absolutely without foundation—"

"That is enough, Mr Walmsford," interrupted Sturt. "This court has been convened to establish cause of death. All this, as far as the court is concerned, is irrelevant."

"Your pardon, sir. I am merely trying to clear the name of a young man who is not able to defend himself."

"And you have done an admirable job. This court agrees that no evidence has been submitted to connect this young man with the person seen at the hotel. The fact that he was wearing similar clothing appears to be mere coincidence. Now, may we get on with the business of this court."

Walmsford sat down, smiling to himself, was immediately in conference with Pyke Senior and his colleague. Steven was told to stand down. The pathologist was called.

While Keene was taking the oath and generally replying to questions of identity. Sturt looked on with pursed lips. As soon as the preliminaries were over he started in on the questioning.

"I notice, Mr Keene, you state death was due to suffocation."

"That is correct."

"In your considered opinion, could he have been suffocated elsewhere, then brought to the chip pile and buried there?"

"Unlikely. Most unlikely. The lungs contained minute fibres of wood that are identical with the beech chips in that pile. I would say categorically he died there."

"He was drunk?"

"No. His blood count was very low. At the most a couple of beers. However, his clothes showed evidence of liquor spill. Which would account for the testimony that he smelled like a wino."

"Your report comments also on the absence of drugs."

"That is correct."

"So we have a young man who is not drunk, who is not under the influence of drugs, burrowing into the chip pile. For what?"

"I have no idea. But the suggestion made by the foreman sounded quite feasible."

Sturt asked a few more questions, finally pronounced his finding, emphasising once again that Cody Pyke was not connected in any way with the incident at the hotel.

Steven smiled wryly. It would appear the main reason for the examination of testimonies, his own and the pathologist's in particular, was to exonerate the deceased.

He signed the typed sheets of his own evidence, pocketed his copy, looked at his watch. Almost on cue a young man was at his side.

"We still have time to catch your plane, sir. We've phoned ahead to confirm the booking."

Steven sighed, thanked him. Together they left the building, climbed into a dark blue Austin. They were travelling along the waterfront road when the driver slowed, stopped behind a white Mini parked awkwardly at the side of the road. He jumped out, hurried along to the woman standing resignedly beside it, spoke to her, looked at the engine, gestured towards the Austin.

Steven watched the little pantomime with casual interest. The woman seemed familiar, tall, slender, golden hair braided and coiled around the small head like a crown, hair that gleamed and glistened in the sun. She nodded, turned to walk back to the car. Steven smiled in satisfaction as he placed a name to those patrician features.

The driver opened the door, explained, "We're giving Mrs Wilson a lift to Gardener's Garage. Okay?"

"Okay," said Steven, turning in his seat as the driver restarted the car. "You're Eden Wilson, aren't you? Edenware Potteries?"

A slight frown creased the smooth forehead but her eyes were hidden behind the dark glasses. "Yes. I'm Eden Wilson."

"Thought so. You wouldn't remember me—but my wife and I were out at your place last weekend. We bought a coffee set and admired that piece you call Petal."

Mrs Wilson nodded politely. "Of course. I'm sorry I didn't recognise you before but I see so many people casually like that. What are you doing back so soon?"

15

"Business this time. I hoped to go out to Edenware before I left but I was tied up all day. What I wanted to know is whether the Petal is still available."

She hesitated. "You're from Wellington somewhere, aren't you?"

"Somewhere," Steven agreed. "Lower Hutt to be exact."

The woman looked relieved. "That's good then. Because we do still have the Petal bowl but it's not for sale right now."

She smiled teasingly at his dismay. "It's all right. Edenware is holding a one day exhibition and sale in Lower Hutt next Saturday, 17th. Thorncliff Hall, Mitchell Street. D'you know it? We are showing Petal, of course, so it's packed away right now. But afterwards, well, you could pick it up then. That suit you?"

Steven laughed. "Wonderful. And my wife will be delighted to have another look at your stuff." He tore a sheet of paper from his notebook, scrawled "Steven Arrow, $10 deposit", attached a $10 note and handed it over as the car stopped by the garage.

Mrs Wilson climbed out, thanked the driver and they were on their way again. "That was a stroke of luck," gloated Steven. "My last instructions—get that doodah or else."

They reached the terminal with barely ten minutes to spare. Steven spent the first part of the short flight sorting out notes for the report he would have to submit to Jonas—Detective Chief Inspector Jonas Peacock. Steven's boss. And Kylie's uncle. Jonas had considered Steven's summons to the inquest totally unnecessary, had muttered about young officers shirking, but the summons was there, could not be ignored.

For that reason alone, Steven knew his report would have to be without fault. Fortunately this afternoon Jonas was attending a meeting of District Chiefs. The report could wait till morning. Wondering idly who had replaced him as general dogsbody, Steven put his notes back into his pocket, glanced down at Marlborough Sound's pattern of dark green hills, deep blue sea.

Brown fire breaks and climbing access roads scarred the living green of the hills. Any little cove showing signs of habitation had its own marina. Launches painted white arrowheads on the sheltered waters. Presently they were over the choppy open water of the Strait, the hostess was telling everyone to fasten seat belts as they were coming in to land at Wellington.

Steven hurried from the plane to the reception area, found Kylie after a brief search, told her of his success in reserving the Petal bowl. As far as they were concerned, his trip to Nelson had not been a complete waste of time.

Tuesday morning he had barely finished his report when Peacock walked into the small office. He nodded curtly to Steven's bright "Good morning", settled down in his big chair, began pulling papers out of drawers, placing them on the top of his desk. He took an extraordinarily long time to peruse the daily police report, even went through the ritual of unwrapping a stick of gum and thoroughly masticating it before he deigned to look across at Steven.

"Right," he said. "Tell me about it. Not the official guff. The background bits and pieces. Especially why it was so important you attended. A routine inquest, wasn't it?"

"Well, there was a reason," Steven said quietly. Briefly he outlined everything, including Fairbrother's disclosures. Jonas listened intently for all the fact he professed disinterest.

"Accident, eh? What d'you think?"

"On the evidence given, the only finding possible."

Peacock snarled. "That's not what I asked. I want to know what you think. You. A copper. A suspicious copper. The guy who's supposed to be protecting the public and all that guff. So give. Your opinion. Your own gut feeling."

Steven looked at the fierce eyes, the bristling brows, looked down at his desk, ventured, "I think it was murder."

"Can you prove it?"

"No. But all the facts—"

"What facts? A man roughed up in a car park. A body in the chip pile. Wearing the same outf.t. Those your facts?"

"Well, yes, but even you can see the connection—"

"Can I? The way you dished it out, yeh, maybe. But don't forget—this time we're on the outside looking in. We know some facts. Not all the facts. Nelson investigated. Nelson said accident. Advised the coroner. They had all the facts. All of them. And you—with only some of the facts—you come along—an outsider—"

He stopped as the telephone whirred. Jonas scowled at the interruption, picked up the receiver, spoke briefly.

He hung up, smiled wryly. "All right. Forget about Nelson. Forget about the chip pile. We've got a murder of our own to handle. A murder. Obvious. No holds barred. Shopkeeper found dead in his shop with his head bashed in. Over at the Wainui Mall."

CHAPTER II

WAINUI, A CITY of 21,000 people, was on the other side of the eastern hills, that enclosed the Hutt Valley. A dormitory city with meagre industry, it was policed from Lower Hutt—periodic sweeps by two-man patrol cars—and one resident policeman. That sounded little enough, but an emergency call would send a fleet of cars to stop a riot, a raft of specialised personnel to solve a murder.

The only access road snaked up the eastern hills, dropped down the other side, straightened to become the main road across the floor of the valley, passing through new subdivisions, through the original settlement affectionately called "the Village", through park and farmland right out to the wild and barren coast.

In 1970 a shopping mall was built opposite the Community Centre, between Queen Street and the Strand, a shopping area that supplemented the shops in Queen Street and on the Main Road at the Village. Thirty-four shops in all shapes and sizes, from large supermarkets to small intimate knick-knack shops such as the one where the body of Carter Montgomery Ancell had been found.

Steven turned the car south-east towards the Wainui Hill, Peacock beside him, thumbing through the terse reports they had already received. There were roadworks on the lower slopes, but they soon left these behind as they swept up the wide road to the summit. One last glance towards the silver-blue waters of Wellington Harbour moving lazily under the hot sun and they were over the top, on the shorter road descending into the valley.

Native bush grew above them on the right, dark green, washed by random patches of thin white where manuka bloomed late. On the left, the ground dropped away so sharply that tall trees growing on the steep slope below showed only their feathery tops above road level. The floor of the valley seemed to be covered with houses, wooden bungalow-type, colourful, each with its own section of carefully-tended green.

18

The car came off the hill, proceeded down the wide main stretch, turned left at the Baptist Church onto the Strand, a narrow street that curved around past the shopping mall.

Steven stopped the car outside the patrol base situated less than a hundred yards away. The uniform man waiting in the doorway saluted as they climbed out, came forward.

"Driscoll, sir," he introduced himself. "You said you wanted to use the base for operations."

"That's right, Driscoll." Peacock glanced briefly at the Mall—serene and white, bright pennants flying—followed the local man into the base.

He stopped in the doorway of the main inner room, looked around in satisfaction at the clean, uncluttered look, four desks each with telephone, typewriter. "Yes, it will do nicely. All right, Driscoll, bring us up to date."

Driscoll walked over to the far wall where a plan of the Mall had been pinned.

Police Constable John Harlan Driscoll. People's cop. Community liaison officer. These were the labels given him by newspapers. His beat the whole valley, his office the patrol base, which had been built in 1977 primarily to provide a calling point for the patrol cars until it was decided a permanent police presence was also necessary.

Hence Driscoll. His job: to talk to people, to know people, to be known. An intelligent choice. He was family, had been a resident for over twenty years. A capable man but he could go only so far. As today. Carter Ancell had been found murdered so Lower Hutt sent men, equipment. Driscoll slipped naturally into his important role of local-information officer.

He began by explaining the layout of the Mall—thirty-four shops set around a promotion court shaped like a Latin cross, public exits at each tip of the cross. Most shops had back doors to enable unloading supplies. Ancell's Gifts and Novelties, one of the smaller shops, had no outside exit, only a front door that opened directly on to the central promotion court.

North of the complex was an extensive car park bordered by a plant nursery and showroom—south, an even larger car park. Beyond that were houses which had been there when the Mall was built.

"Burglar alarms?" Peacock asked crisply.

"Perimeter alarm. Contact-operated. Switched on when the manager leaves. Switched off when he comes in. Bypass switch at each public entrance. Each shoppie has own switch-key. Gives him fifty seconds to enter and re-engage the alarm."

"Ancell's shop?"

Driscoll pointed to the small shop marked "A" on the plan—set on the south side between a cake kitchen and an electrical appliance store. "Completely within the confines of the Mall. No personal exit door."

"Right. Now you found Ancell?"

Driscoll moved over to another plan hastily-drawn to show detail of Ancell's Gifts and Novelties—an oblong divided into three sections, main shop and display area, behind it a small workshop adjoining an even smaller office.

"Ancell was found here. In the workshop. Found by his assistant, a Mrs Teresa Martin. She arrived a few minutes after nine, found shop closed. Didn't take too much notice of that, she says. If Ancell leaves the shop for a few minutes he always locks up. She used her own key, went into the office, put her purse on the desk there. Her first job was pricing some items of costume jewellery. She went into the workshop—the safe's there—and found Ancell. Didn't touch anything, she says. Went straight into the electrical shop next door, told the owner, Hugo Benson. He had a look, notified the Mall manager, Gerrard Townsend. He called me in."

He stopped talking, looked at Peacock, who shook his head impatiently. "Well, what then. Didn't stop there, did you?"

"No, sir. I could see he was dead but I asked Dr Brooker of the Health Centre to confirm." He waved a vague hand. Steven remembered noticing the Health Centre on the west side of the Strand.

"Dr Brooker said cerebral haemorrhage. A blunt instrument. Happened last night some time but beyond that he wouldn't go. Said he was only a GP. Out of practice."

"No matter. We'll get a closer time later. And then?"

"I sealed the area, notified Lower Hutt. The scene squad arrived about half an hour ago."

Peacock nodded. "This Ancell. Tell me about him."

"In his fifties. Unmarried. Lay preacher. The Baptist Church. You passed it on the way in. Very civic-minded. Community-oriented. Highly thought of by everyone even though he's inclined to be a bit testy at times. Had a shop on Queen Street for years, shifted into the Mall when it opened. His nephew, Luke Ancell, worked with him until middle January this year. Since then been managing with Mrs Martin, nine till four."

"D'you know why Luke Ancell left?"

"Some say a real stand-up fight. Others think just Carter Ancell being a mite high-handed." He paused. "Generation gap probably. Luke's his stepbrother's son. Only child. Parents killed in car crash two years this March. Luke's father an absolute no-good. No form but—womaniser—gambler. Real no-hoper. Just the opposite to Carter. Luke—well, I'd say Luke was drifting into the same pattern. Until Carter took over. Made him work for him."

"Know where he's working now?"

"No. No one seems to know. Maybe he's not working. Hoping Carter will take him back."

"And Mrs Martin?"

"Nice woman. Widow. Husband killed in that chemical blow-out at ICI. Late forties. Good reputation."

Peacock nodded, stood up, moved towards the door. "Well, scene squad should have something to tell us by now. Let's go."

They left the base, walked in silence to the Mall. Already people were gathering, mostly young women with children, colourful sun-dresses, separates. They stood in little groups, watching the uniform man guarding the western entrance.

He saluted when he saw Peacock, opened the door he was standing by, one of three swing doors set into the glass wall terminating the longer leg of the promotion court. The immediate area had been closed off—the swing door on the far right locked, a rope barrier extending from glass wall to past the cake kitchen.

There were people standing around in the open area, curious, watchful, quiet. The uniform man on guard at the shop lifted the rope barrier to let the police party through, refastened it.

Driscoll opened the door onto an Aladdin's cave. Wide plate-glass shelves on the left displayed ornamental crystal, silver, ceramics. On the right were utility items, glass, silver, china. Along the centre, waist-high cabinets were stocked with craft material, glittering in massed anonymity.

At the back of the shop, two archways led to office and workshop. Immediately in front, a shop-wide counter showed costume jewellery. The wall between the two archways was half mirror, half pegboard bedecked with fashion pieces.

Detective Sergeant David Galt came forward, led them behind the long counter, past the office archway into the workshop. The body of Carter Ancell lay near the open door of the safe, face downward, dark navy suit, longish hair curling at the nape of his neck, silver-grey except for the death area soaked with blood—

thick, dark, congealed. His outstretched hands were clawed, tiny marks on the rubber flooring showing where his scrabbling fingers had tried desperately to hold on to life.

The small room was singularly neat except for the body. Half the width of the shop, six feet deep, little space for any fittings other than a narrow bench on the side opposite the doorway, drawers underneath on the left, safe fitted partly under on the right. There was a rack above with pint-sized tools, none of which appeared to be missing. The bench itself was clear.

No windows. Strip lighting bathed the scene with harsh white glare, touched the hair of the murdered man with gleams of silver.

Peacock leaned over the body, pushed the safe door open wider with a finger covered by a handkerchief. Three shelves—two holding books and papers, the top shelf empty except for two silver chain necklaces. The bottom was crowded with glass jars, sheets of metal.

"Dr Whittaker been yet?" Peacock asked, straightening.

"Yes, sir. Says between nine and eleven, even twelve. Ancell took anything up to an hour—an hour and a half—to die." Galt's lips twisted. "Pity the alarm wasn't triggered. Doc thinks they could've saved him if they'd got to him in time."

"Found his keys?"

"Not yet. Nor a wooden mallet that should be on the bench. Benson next door told us about the mallet. Usually left on the bench just there."

"The mallet being the blunt instrument?"

"Possible. Heavy teak head with a bit of suede tacked on." Galt waved his hand towards the crammed shelves in the shop. "Doesn't look like a burglary, does it? Looks more like Ancell brought someone in. They quarrelled. Ancell was clobbered. The other guy let himself out by the key-switch. On fifty-second delay, they tell me."

Peacock nodded absently, looked around once more. "We'll be down in the manager's office if you want me."

They came out of the shop to find a short plump man with an anxious creased face talking to the constable. He gave them a relieved smile when he was introduced as the manager, Gerrard Townsend, explained that Mrs Martin was waiting to be questioned in his office. She seemed to have recovered from the initial shock, wanted to talk. Perhaps if they could see her now?

Peacock nodded genially, followed the manager along the long leg of the promotion court, seemingly unaware of curious glances.

They turned left into the cross passage, right again into a darker corridor tucked behind the large Book and Toy Centre.

They walked through the tiny reception area into the manager's office where two women were sitting, talking in muted whispers. The one dressed in a blue trouser suit withdrew discreetly at Townsend's nod.

He introduced the police officers to Mrs Martin—faded, motherly, blue eyes and brown hair, cream cardigan over a pale green dress. She steeled herself visibly, waited for the martyr's axe to fall.

Peacock sat down opposite her, said kindly, "We realise you've had a great shock, Mrs Martin, so we won't keep you long. But we do need to know what happened. If you tell us every detail you can remember, we'll have one of our men along to get a signed statement from you later. That all right?"

Teresa Martin nodded, smoothed her skirt with absent fingers, began hesitantly. "I came in at my usual time. I get the bus to the Mall because I live way down Wellington Road and the bus gets to Queen Street about five to nine. I came in the Queen Street entrance like I always do. Went straight to the shop. It was locked —I mean, the door was locked and the closed sign showing. That's not unusual. If Mr Ancell has to go out—even for a few minutes— he always locks up. That's why I have a key of my own. Anyway, I opened the door and went inside. Everything looked quite normal and I went into the office—that's the little room at the back next— next to the workroom. I put my purse down—looked around to see if Mr Ancell had left any instructions. He—he usually does. Little notes of anything as he thinks of it and I'm not around to tell. Well, there were a couple of invoices pinned to the pad so I knew some stuff had come in and he wanted me to do the pricing. I went into the workroom and—and—"

She stopped, pressed her crumpled handkerchief against quivering lips, closed her eyes momentarily, shook herself, ploughed on resolutely.

"Mr Ancell was there. Lying on the floor. And his head! It was ghastly. I don't know what happened next exactly. I think I just stood there for a while—y'know, not believing what I was seeing. I know I didn't scream or anything. I guess I was too shocked to move. Then—then I sort of pulled myself together and went into Mr Benson next door and told him—about it—and he—well, he took over from there." She looked at Peacock shyly. "I didn't scream or anything. Not a peep."

She seemed inordinately proud of the fact that she had not

23

screamed. Peacock leaned forward, patted her on the shoulder, commending her for her level-headed behaviour.

A sudden rush of colour stained the pale cheeks, her eyes brightened, whether with unshed tears or simply because of the gentle praise, Steven could not tell. He recognised Mrs Martin was still in a state of mild shock, would only too soon be hit with the sudden realisation of what had actually happened.

"Well, that's given us a fairly clear picture, Mrs Martin," said Peacock quietly. "But there are one or two questions we need to ask. For instance, you said those invoices let you know some stuff had come in. Whose invoices?"

"Oh, didn't I say? They were Delacourt invoices. The costume jewellery people. Over in the Hutt there. Mr Ancell gets most of his stuff from them. Trinkets and so on."

"So you went into the workroom to . . .?"

"Well, I knew Mr Ancell would check them out and put them in the safe. I went in to get them, of course."

"You have a key to the safe?"

"Oh, no. Mr Ancell keeps the key—" She hesitated, looked at them sharply. "The safe was open, wasn't it? The key in the lock. I remember now. I didn't think I'd noticed anything much but I remember—the safe was open. Does that mean . . .?"

Peacock did not make any comment. He allowed her to think back, think back to everything she had noticed, consciously, subconsciously.

"Mr Ancell would've put them in the safe. On the top shelf. They aren't there, are they? But they weren't all that valuable, Inspector. Not worth killing a man for. Nobody would kill—at least—" Her voice trailed away, eyes distant, unbelieving.

"Yes, it would seem the Delacourt delivery has gone. They would be worth—say a few hundred maybe?"

"Easily. Retail. What the trade calls impulse-buying stuff. Not too dear but attractive."

"Have you any idea what was in that consignment?"

Mrs Martin fidgeted. "Well, the invoices—I never really got to see them—but they'll tell you. Brooches mainly. Bracelets. Depends on how much of the order was filled."

Peacock nodded. "There is one other thing, Mrs Martin. You started to say where Mr Ancell kept the key—"

Mrs Martin flushed prettily. "The key was kept in the slide drawer under the bench. I—I know that doesn't sound too good from the security angle but—well, the only things that got into the

24

safe were items that still had to be priced. Once they were priced they went on display. Mr Ancell used the safe mainly as an extra cupboard."

Peacock smiled. "When you say Mr Ancell, you mean Carter Ancell. We understand there's a nephew. Luke Ancell. They quarrelled, I believe."

Mrs Martin eyed him warily, lips tight. "Well, I don't know what happened exactly. Young Luke—well, Mr Ancell was grooming him to take over the shop. He kept talking of retiring in a couple of years. But a few weeks ago—yes, they quarrelled and Luke took off. Hasn't been near his uncle since."

"D'you know Luke's address? Or where he works?"

"I don't know where he works now, but he has a flat down in the Village. It's—" She stopped, looked squarely at Peacock. "You don't think young Luke had anything to do with this, Inspector? I mean, they may have quarrelled like I said—but Luke—Luke wouldn't hurt his uncle."

"Well, you know Luke better than we do but we still have to notify him of his uncle's death. Routine. It's quite possible Luke is Carter Ancell's only living relative."

"Yes, I think he is. Luke's parents were killed a couple of years ago. In a car crash."

She frowned, said accusingly, "You do think Luke has something to do with this, don't you?"

"We don't think anything right now, Mrs Martin. At present it looks as though Mr Ancell disturbed a burglar. Certainly a robbery seems to have taken place. But we are still only at the beginning of our investigations."

Mrs Martin accepted the explanation without question, supplied Luke's address. Steven, watching her face, wondered how long it would be before she worked out for herself that Peacock was being deliberately evasive.

Peacock smiled easily. "Well, Mrs Martin, Sergeant Arrow will drive you home now. And tomorrow we'd like you to come in and work out if anything else is missing. Think you can do that?"

"Yes, of course. It's just a matter of setting the sales slips against the inward invoices. We have a system, y'know. We mark the daily sales in a special re-ordering book so we don't run out of the better-selling lines."

"Very good, Mrs Martin. We'll see you again tomorrow then." He looked at Steven with raised eyebrows. Steven jumped up, hurried back to the patrol base, brought the car around to the northern entrance, returned to the office to find Peacock deep in conversation with the manager, Mrs Martin once more in the care of the secretary.

"Have you everything, Mrs Martin?" he asked quietly. "Your purse and so on?"

"Yes, it's all here. First thing I grabbed. Sort of reflex action, y'know." She stood up, expressed her thanks to the secretary, followed Steven out to the car.

"Is there anyone you'd like me to get in touch with for you?" Steven asked as he settled her in the car. "We don't like to leave anyone alone when they've had an experience such as yours."

Mrs Martin smiled tiredly. "My sister lives with me, Sergeant. I phoned her as soon as I knew you were taking me home."

Relieved, Steven drove his silent passenger to the town-house type of dwelling on Wellington Road, handed her over to the tall, scrawny woman waiting at the front door.

His next call was to the flats where Luke Ancell lived. Situated on the other side of the Village, they were stepped up the side of a low hill—which meant they lost the afternoon sun early in the day.

Steven looked disapprovingly at the grey-painted building with its jaded cemented-in look. The area immediately around was tarsealed, marked out for parking, with the usual row of letter box/milk box at the edge of the footpath. Most had several pieces of familiar junk mail sticking out of the slot, including Luke's letter box "G", which also sported a clasp and snap-lock, the only one in the whole row.

Steven entered a tiled hall which had once been bright and cheerful. Now it was sad and grimy, overlaid with a thin veneer of constant neglect.

He knocked on the door of 273G not expecting anyone to answer. After a pause he tried other flats. Finally he found a woman home in 273D, puffy-eyed, greasy-haired, untidy.

"What d'you want?" she asked suspiciously.

"I'm looking for Mr Ancell, flat G. He doesn't appear to be home. D'you know where he works? I need to speak to him urgently."

"He's got a shop in the Mall, hasn't he?" Sullenly.

"He used to work there but he changed his job recently." When the woman continued to look blankly at him, he asked. "Is it likely anyone else might know where he works?"

The woman shrugged. "Not likely. Keeps himself to himself,

does Mr High-and-mighty Ancell. Doesn't talk to the likes of us. And as for letting anyone know he'd lost his job—" She laughed derisively.

"Well, if you do see him tonight, will you tell him to get in touch with the manager of the Mall, please?"

"Mightn't come home," she said sharply. "Doesn't always. No, you'd better come around yourself if you want to get that message to him. Or leave a note in his letter box. Chances are he won't be home tonight anyway."

"Was he home last night, do you know?"

"Nope. Lit out after nine some time. Been doing that lately. I mean, going off at odd hours. Staying away for days. I know. Because he parks that new car of his right under my window. Like as not leaves in the early hours of the morning. Comes back late."

Steven thanked her, left the building.

He paused by the row of letter boxes, wrote a note, slipped it into box G, all the time aware of sharp eyes watching him through flimsy curtains.

When he stopped the car in front of the patrol base, he noticed an ambulance pulled up in front of the Mall entrance, Driscoll keeping the area clear of spectators. He went into the base to find Mat Ruakere unpacking a large cardboard box.

"Know where the boss is?" he asked.

"Still with the Mall manager, I think, Sarge." Ruakere hardly paused in his task of giving each desk its required quota of paper.

Steven left the base, walked over to the Mall as the ambulance was pulling away. Curious eyes followed him as he went through the swing door, the door that had previously been locked, was now wide open. The rope barrier had been removed from the glass wall.

Everything was back to normal except for the uniform man in front of Ancell's Gifts and Novelties. Newly-arrived shoppers paused to gaze at the shop, wandered off again. There was nothing to see. Inside, behind the closed door, men were still busy, intent on finding those small pieces of evidence that might some day build into a case against a murderer.

CHAPTER III

STEVEN TRAVERSED the long leg of the promotion court, turned the corner, nearly ran into Peacock.

"Oh, you're back. Good! Come with me." Peacock made an abrupt about turn, headed for the northern entrance to the Mall, the same glass wall, but double swing doors instead of the three at other entrances. They stepped out on to the northern car park, looked around the vast empty space. No cars allowed meantime.

Peacock said, "Townsend's been quite informative. Given me thumbnail sketches of everyone. Including such interesting items as the number of *de facto* marriages and the fact that Hugo Benson, a widower, dyes his hair. All one great big family, he says."

"More murders are committed within the family group than anywhere else," said Steven grimly.

"Yeh, I know. Now, the plant nursery closes at the same time as the other shops, five-thirty. The Tavern, on the other hand, doesn't close till 10 p.m." Peacock pointed to the long low building almost directly opposite the plant nursery. Except for the Health Centre, it was the only structure on that side of the Strand, the area around being laid out in playing fields and a proposed park area. "Maybe someone there saw something. You know the routine."

Steven knew the routine. Talk to the manager, the barman, list names of people they remembered, then ask each of those to name the people he remembered until they had a fairly composite picture of who had been at the Tavern last night.

After all that work, after interviewing everyone anyone could remember, probably no one would have noticed anything unusual going on around the Mall anyway. Still, it had to be done.

Peacock stood in the sun gazing at the backs of the Queen Street shops which formed the eastern boundary of the car park.

"Queen Street shops. Have to take them in as well. Shops closed but maybe some conscientious person working late. Maybe. Did you locate Luke Ancell?"

"Not at home. Nobody knows where he's working."

"Oh, well, early days. Put out a broadcast for him. If he doesn't answer—" He paused. "Come along. Let's have a look at the other car park."

He turned abruptly, re-entered the Mall, this time walking straight across to the opposite entrance. This car park was easily twice as large as the other one, houses to the south, open area towards the Strand.

Two direct entrances came in from the main road, one running along the back of the Queen Street shops to the east—a service lane—the other almost in line with the point where they stood.

"Ancell doesn't use his car overmuch," said Peacock abruptly. "Lives too close. So we're not going to get anyone telling us they heard a car come in here around nine or ten or what-have-you. And anyone using these entrances, especially that service lane behind the shops there, would hardly be noticed. But do a house-to-house anyhow. Jack that up?"

"Yes, sir," said Steven. It was routine, already in progress, although Steven carefully did not mention it. Unfortunately, all the houses faced the main road, had high back fences with tall crowding trees, thick bushes, shielding them from the Mall car park. Unless some householder happened to be down at the back of his quarter acre for some obscure reason they were not likely to learn anything much from there either.

"Might as well open up the car parks now. Not serving any purpose keeping them closed." Peacock turned quickly on his heel. "Come along. Want to see Benson before lunch."

Back in the Mall, they walked up the long leg to the shop next to Ancell's Gifts and Novelties. Hugo Benson was serving a customer—or at least talking to one. When he saw Peacock and Steven, he stopped, signalled to an assistant, came over to greet them.

"You'll be wanting to talk to me, I'll wager. Come into my office." He turned, led the way. Hugo Benson was overweight, jowly, sharp brown eyes under heavy dark brows, thick thatch of black hair. He closed the door behind them, perched on the edge of the narrow built-in desk, began talking even before the police officers settled in two chairs that took up most of the remaining space.

"Fair shook me up, that did. Old Ancell. Never did anybody any harm in his whole life, I'll bet. Quiet. Good citizen. Y'know. And that's how he finishes. Makes you wonder what the world's coming to. All this violence. Nobody's safe any more. Nobody!"

"You knew Carter Ancell fairly well?"

"We—ell. Didn't socialise, if that's what you mean. Different interests. He's church. Me—I'm more for sport. Committees. That sort of thing. But we're a close-knit bunch here. Y'know. Can't help it really. Thrown together more or less. And anything—well, anything off-beat—soon got around."

"What exactly d'you mean by off-beat, Mr Benson?"

"Nothing criminal, Inspector. Nothing like that. Mostly petty things. Tattle. That sort of thing."

"Was there tattle about Ancell?"

"We—ell. He was a mite mean. No, not really mean. Just watched his pennies, y'know. That's why he and Luke—" He stopped abruptly, bit his lip in vexation.

"That's why he and Luke quarrelled? Is that what you were going to say, Mr Benson? We already know about the quarrel."

Benson looked uncomfortable. "Do you now? Well, yes, they did quarrel. Young Luke wanted to expand. Spread out a bit. A bigger shop coming vacant end of March. Luke wanted to take over but Carter—well, he held the purse-strings. Kept reminding Luke, y'know. Made Luke madder than hell. I tried to get Carter to see what Luke was getting at but he closed up. Said none of my business. Guess he was right at that."

"You say Carter held the purse-strings. What did Luke put into the business?"

"Well, not money, anyway. And what he knows Carter taught him. A bright boy though. A real asset."

"How long have you known Carter Ancell, Mr Benson?"

"Oh, around twenty years or so. We both had shops in Queen Street before we transferred to the Mall."

"And Luke?"

"Well, only since he joined Carter. Five years ago?"

"When he was around nineteen?"

"Yeh. Thereabouts. Luke's father was a bit of a waster, y'know. Got himself into trouble moneywise at the drop of a hat. Carter bailed him out a couple of times, that I do know. Luke looked like he was heading the same way. Job-jumping. Drifting. Only Carter took over. Sat on him. Made him shape up. Done a good job on the boy, I reckon."

Peacock nodded. "We've been trying to contact Luke Ancell, Mr Benson. He's not at home and nobody seems to know where he's working right now. D'you know?"

Benson shook his head slowly. "No. Haven't seen him since he quit. Haven't heard about him either, oddly enough. Of course, Carter wouldn't say anything. But usually someone knows."

"But not this time?"

"No, not this time."

"If you do hear anything, we'd be grateful for the information. Now, what time did you leave the Mall last night?"

"Around six-thirty, I guess. One or two things I had to tidy up."

"Before or after Carter Ancell?"

"After. Well after. Carter had a church meeting. Goes home pretty smartly then. A bite to eat, y'know, before the meeting."

"Did he mention coming back to the shop?"

"Not to me, he didn't. Wasn't the type. Kept his own counsel, y'know. Expected everyone else to be the same."

"And you, Mr Benson. What were you doing last night?"

"Me? Babysitting. My daughter and her hubby went into Wellington for the Val Doonican show. Got me to hold the fort."

Peacock left it at that. There would be other opportunities to talk to Benson. A break now might allow him to remember something he had omitted to tell them. Perhaps.

As they left the shop Peacock told Steven he had to go to the Hutt, would be back about three. Steven walked with him to the patrol base, watched him drive off in the police car.

Inside the base, Steven found a small crowd of men, plain clothes and uniform, men brought in from Lower Hutt to assist in the matter of Carter Ancell. They were grouped around Driscoll, waiting for the jug to boil as they sampled sandwiches they had brought from home or purchased from one of the Mall lunch counters.

Seats were at a premium but he found a space next to David Galt on the edge of a desk, began pumping David about scene squad activities. Most of it was negative.

No keys had been found on Ancell or anywhere in the shop. Yet he needed a key to bypass the burglar alarm. Ergo, whoever had bashed Ancell had taken the keys to make sure the alarm was not tripped when he left. Neither had they located the mallet, the probable blunt instrument. No sign either of the consignment of fashion jewellery.

David had seen the Delacourt invoices, the kind that were made out at the same time as delivery docket, stock release, office copy. All the items on the invoices had been ticked, suggesting Ancell had unpacked the consignment, checked it before putting the containers into the safe.

The value of the consignment was $375, according to the invoices.

Little enough it seemed when there was so much of greater value in the shop itself. Either the thief had taken fright after slamming Ancell or, as seemed more and more likely, the Delacourt stuff had been taken as a cover.

Their conversation was interrupted by Detective Constable Tai Bennett who plumped himself down beside Steven, rubbed his face with his big hands.

"God Almighty! Some of these dames! They certainly know how to lay it out for you, don't they?"

Steven and David looked at each other, grinned sardonically.

"Come on, Tai," said David chidingly. "You're a big boy now. Should be able to handle that kind of situation easily. What's she like? Lush—or a no-hoper?"

Tai grimaced, waved his hands in a woman shape. "Lush, I guess. Over-ripe. Full blown. Offering everything on a plate. But when she's old enough to be your mother—"

"Really?" said Steven and David together.

"Well, nearly then," said Tai belligerently. "Never been so embarrassed in all my life. Coming on like that. Like I was there for her benefit. And all those younger chicks—watching—grinning—"

"What d'you mean?" Steven demanded. "Younger chicks watching? What younger chicks?"

"Y'know. In the fashion shop. This dame was on my list for questioning. Took me into this office kind of thing at the back of the store. Windows all around. Everyone could look in. And did they look in! Seen that kind of show before, I reckon."

Steven chuckled. "Let me guess. The red-haired bint with heavy make-up. Wears those slinky dresses. Too short. Too low."

"You've guessed it. Name of Sheila Bungay. Some sheila! How'd you like her coming on hot and strong like that? Must be forty if she's a day."

The others simply laughed, gleefully, delightedly, until Tai grinned sheepishly back, brown eyes glinting with shy amazement.

"All right," said Steven at last. "Joking aside. Did you get any-thing worthwhile out of her?"

"Different, anyway. Only one I've come across didn't like old man Ancell. Bad tempered, she says. Shifty. Never looks you straight in the eye."

"Anyone? Or just her?" interposed Steven.

"Can you blame him," chimed in David. "All that woman being thrown at him while he was trying to think about what he was saying."

Tai shrugged. "Well, that's her story. The others liked Ancell.
A bit pious maybe. But heart of gold. Do anything for you. Help-
ing hand in time of need and all the rest of it. But this female!
Says he's a nasty type. Always fighting with someone. Trivial
matters mostly. And not the shouting yelling kind of fighting, either.
The cold hard-voiced nasty kind."

"D'you think she had a thing for Luke?"

"Yeh, maybe that's it. Talked about this Luke like he was something out of this world. Said Carter was forever picking on him.
Trying to show him up in front of others. She couldn't even pass the
time of day without Carter butting in."

"Maybe he was just guarding the boy's morals."

"Yeh. According to her, he'd be the type."

"Maybe he had a point. Look how you reacted."

"Cripes! How old is this Luke anyway? She talked like he was
a bit of a kid but my info is he's around twenty-four or so. Old
enough to make his own mistakes without Uncle Carter butting
in."

"He's twenty-four all right. Did she know where he's working?"

"Nope. Says no one does. Got her own ideas though. Thinks he
hasn't got a job. Saw him driving around couple of days ago. Maybe
hoping to get back with Carter."

"Maybe. Did she say anything about the quarrel?"

"Well, she walked in on them one day—snarling at each other.
Clammed up straight away. Both of them. But you could cut the
atmosphere with a knife. Luke white and tense. Carter calm and
spiteful. He pushed Luke into the workroom. Attended to her himself. Unusual, she says. Luke always did the shop bit."

"And just after that Luke lit out?"

"Oh, no. A good week later. Another fight probably."

"She says Ancell was quarrelsome. Everyone? Or just Luke?"

"Everyone, seems like. This meeting they have once a month.
Advertising, promotion and such. All the Mall shoppies attend.
Ancell always sticks his oar in. Especially when anything advanced
or really mod suggested. Then he had a flaming row with Benson—"

"Benson? The owner of the electrical store?"

"Yes. She thought it was probably something to do with Luke.
Maybe Benson tried to smooth things over. Carter wouldn't take
too kindly to that, I'd guess."

"Doesn't seem a good enough reason. Unless Ancell was one of
those touchy people who flare up over nothing."

"Sounds like he was. Maybe the others being a mite careful.

33

Don't want to talk ill of the dead. But this one—strikes me she thinks being outspoken's next best to being noticed."

Steven picked up some of the reports. Nothing in them suggested Ancell was cantankerous. Even Townsend, in his nutshell character analyses for Peacock, had been close to admiring the old man. "Direct" was an adjective he used. Could be interpreted for or against.

Frank—yes, perhaps. A frank answer sometimes ruffled vanity's feathers. But he had also used words like "understanding"—"generous"—"patient". Now, someone said quarrelsome. Ill-tempered. Maybe it was only the beginning, the first rift in the cocoon of polite murmurings that inevitably surrounded the name of the dead.

Peacock returned at three. Steven reported that Reverend Andrew Bartlett of the Baptist Church was in Wellington, was not expected home till around five. Together they went over all the scraps of information and non-information so far gathered by the interviews.

At three-thirty, Driscoll escorted into the base a pale, frightened-looking woman carrying a paper bag. Driscoll introduced her as Mrs Carpenter, settled her into a chair opposite Peacock, took the paper bag, set it on the desk, opened it by tearing one side.

Peacock stared at the contents—a bunch of keys on a key ring and a wooden mallet with a scrap of chamois tacked on to the head.

"Well, well," he said softly. "Suppose you tell me about it, Mrs Carpenter."

The woman gulped, plunged into her tale. She lived in one of the houses backing on to the Mall car park. She had not found the keys and mallet. Her son, aged four and a half, had found them. He had a little fort at the bottom of the section up against the fence. There were trees growing thick there—ngaio, taupata, native fuschia. From the Mall side it looked like a thick hedge, but behind the galvanised iron the lower parts of the shrubs were quite thin, a gap between them and the fence.

Peter had his fort there—his favourite playing place. It was warm and sheltered and he could crawl back and forth under the branches all along the back of the section.

He went to kindergarten this morning but after lunch he went down to play in his fort. He found the keys first. He knew keys were important so he brought them up to the house. There was a metal tag on the key ring—see—with instructions to ring a certain number if found. She rang this number several times without success, was on the point of ringing Mr Driscoll when Peter came into the house with the mallet.

As soon as she saw the mallet she remembered the man killed in the Mall. She asked a neighbour to mind Peter, put the things into a paper bag and brought them to Mr Driscoll.

"Very good, Mrs Carpenter," said Peacock. "They definitely seem to be items we are looking for in relation to Mr Ancell's death. We are extremely grateful to you."

He explained the fort area would have to be examined closely as soon as possible. In fact, it might be a good idea if she showed Driscoll exactly where it was so he could have a look around now. As soon as the door closed on the unlikely pair, Peacock hooked a Biro through the key ring, lifted it in the air.

"Car keys. Back door. Front door. Bypass switch key. What d'you reckon? Any fingerprints?"

"Doubtful. All that handling. Still—"

Still—they had to be sure.

It was well after four when they set out to have a look at Carter Ancell's house. They walked through the Mall, still crowded with shoppers, came out on to the Queen Street entrance. Queen Street, the outermost curve of a quarter circle. Shops lined the rim, flanked by footpath, roadway, the inner segment of lawn and garden housing the Community Centre, a solid brick building with children's playing area close by.

Peacock and Steven turned left, followed the curve to where Queen Street ran into Fitzherbert Road. Ancell's house was directly opposite, modest bungalow type, wooden, cream with green, garage in front. The garden had been allowed to revert to wild-garden, bushes crowding each other, green on green, splashed by an occasional yellow-leafed coprosma.

They stood on the pavement a moment looking at the house then Peacock opened the low gate to the next-door dwelling, went along the short path to the front door, knocked. The door opened to reveal a sunny hallway, a thin-faced woman well past middle age. As soon as they had identified themselves, with the added information that Driscoll had told them her name, Mrs Fulton invited them into the neat front room.

She knew about Mr Ancell, she said. She had been expecting a visit from the police but there was little she could tell them. Mr Ancell was a quiet neighbour, helpful, kind. He did not have many visitors. The only regular one was his nephew, Luke, who came there often until—until—

MURDER AND CHIPS

"Until they quarrelled," prompted Peacock.

Mrs Fulton looked less flustered. "Oh, you know about that. It was dreadful. I mean, the two of them shouting at each other like that. I couldn't believe it. Mr Ancell was always so quiet—and Luke—well, he's such a nice boy—"

"Could you hear what was being said?"

"Well, not what was being said inside the house. Just the raised voices. Then Luke must've opened the back door because I heard him quite clearly—telling Mr Ancell to keep out of his life. Something like that."

"This happened when exactly?"

She looked at her hands, frowned in concentration. "Last Thursday night. About nine o'clock, I'd say. It was between programmes, y'see. I'd just come out to the kitchen to get my husband some ice cream. He likes a plate of ice cream at night. That's when I heard the raised voices. Loud enough for me to hear in my own kitchen. I kind of stood there wondering what it was all about and just then Luke opened the door, said, well, what I told you—and went storming out along the path. He looked awfully upset. Angry, yet sad, too, in an odd way. I don't know how long they'd been—fighting. Y'see, we were watching one of those noisy cop shows. Y'know, cars roaring around. Guns firing. If I hadn't come out into the kitchen just at that time maybe we wouldn't have heard a thing."

"Have you seen Luke visiting his uncle since then?"

"No. Of course, we're not always at home. And we don't watch out that much. Luke could've visited—but the way he looked that night . . . No, I don't think he's been there since."

While they were talking, a large cat walked into the room, sooty-black, snow-white bib and paws. He gave the visitors a disdainful look, settled into the chair next to Steven.

Mrs Fulton smiled. "That's Sox. Mr Ancell's cat. He comes in here during the day—Mr Ancell being away and all. But at night-time—he knows exactly when Mr Ancell is due home, waits for him by the gate. Cats are good company when you live alone, don't you think?"

Peacock politely agreed although Steven knew he had a thing about cats. They went out to the kitchen to study its relation to Ancell's house, explained they would be going into next door to make a brief search—part of a routine investigation.

"I'm glad you told me," she tittered nervously. "Now I know if I see anyone strange in there it won't be burglars anyway."

36

Peacock looked at Steven. Steven knew what he was thinking. Over the past six months the break squad had been plagued by a burglar whose specialty was stealing from houses of the recently deceased, people who lived alone—people like Carter Ancell.

He made no mention of this as he thanked Mrs Fulton for her co-operation, asked her to let them know if she thought of anything else that could be helpful.

As they walked along the path to the back of Ancell's house, Peacock said abruptly, "Burglars, eh? What d'you think?"

"Worth a try, I suppose. But d'you think he'd bother to come over the hill like that?"

Peacock grimaced. "Never know. Could even live over here for all we know. Who's already here we can use?"

"Ruakere? Single. Working for his sergeant's. Might even enjoy having a bit of peace and quiet."

"Right. We'll use him. Driscoll can rustle up a cot of some kind. See about it."

Peacock opened the back door on to a small adequate kitchen, formica-topped breakfast bar and serving bench separating it from the dining room. They looked into the front room, solid furniture, pine-green carpet and drapes. Everything painfully tidy, unused-looking.

The other rooms were a bedroom and a study, one wall covered from floor to ceiling by crowded bookshelves, a comfortable leather armchair close by.

Peacock examined the roll-top desk. It was not locked. He pushed back the top, surveyed the neatly set-out desk pad, clean and white. Pigeon-holes contained bills, paid and unpaid, leaflets, reminders, a few business letters.

In the right-hand slot was a metal cash box, unlocked. He lifted it out, opened it. It contained papers, pale-blue, pad-sized. Peacock lifted one out to examine. In thick black felt tip the letters IOU were printed across. Below this an amount—$3,000—was written, followed by a florid signature—Hugo Benson—and a due date showing repayment was already overdue.

Peacock spread the other sheets of paper over the desk. Twelve of them, all marked IOU in thick black letters, amounts ranging from $500 to $5,000, most showing a clearing tick in bright red. Only three did not carry the tick. The one to Benson now ten days overdue and two others with due dates still a month away, $800 to M. Alafou and $1,000 to I. Tauvao.

He sorted out the paper showing the earliest date. It was signed

37

Andrew Bartlett. Peacock tapped it thoughtfully against his fingers. "Time we had a talk with the Rev. Mr Bartlett, I think. But we need a car. Lives out Moores Valley road, doesn't he?"

He began leafing through the telephone book to check the address while Steven rang the patrol base instructing Ruakere to bring a car around to Carter Ancell's house.

By the time the car arrived, Peacock was ready to leave, an envelope containing the sheaves of blue IOUs in his pocket. Ruakere was briefed on his duties, stayed inside the house as they drove off to confront the Baptist minister.

He was still not yet home. They had turned to leave when a black Escort 1300 pulled into the drive. They waited till the Rev. Andrew Bartlett climbed out, came towards them with inquiring eyes.

Tall, stooped, scholarly, he was surprised and shocked when they told him of Ancell's death. He led the way to his study, tut-tutting, grieving over the great loss to the community.

He settled down behind the wide desk with its scattered papers, still muttering pious regrets. Peacock interrupted abruptly asking when he had last seen Carter Ancell.

Bartlett confirmed that Ancell had attended the meeting the night before. It had finished around 9.30 p.m. He had himself talked to Carter afterwards for a short while, offered to give him a lift home when he realised Carter had not brought his own car. But Carter said he had something to do at the shop. It was simpler to walk from the church to the Mall, go through to Queen Street along to his own place.

Peacock raised his eyebrows at Steven but made no comment. Instead he asked Bartlett for his personal opinion of Carter Ancell.

"A fine man. Modest. Thoughtful. A great loss."

"We've heard he was inclined to be bad-tempered."

The bushy eyebrows nearly met the hairline. "Well, yes, I must confess there were times when he was a bit testy." He looked a little uneasy at thus contradicting himself, adding firmly, "No, I cannot agree that he was bad-tempered. He did occasionally flare up, of course, as any righteous man does when he sees some of the dreadful things that are happening in this fair land of ours. But mostly, yes, mostly he was even-tempered, kindly, generous—very generous in a businesslike way."

Peacock frowned. "Exactly what do you mean by that?"

"Well, Carter Ancell was not a rich man. Moderately well-off, yes, but most of his money was tied up in his business."

Bartlett smiled tightly. "He did support the church most liberally within his means. Then a few years ago we had a liquidity problem. We desperately needed to show $5,000 or lose a far larger sum we were then negotiating for. Carter could not afford to *give* us this money but he offered a bridging loan without interest. Which in these days of astronomical interest rates was quite a saving. We gladly accepted his offer, paid him back when the other money deal was finalised."

Peacock pulled out the envelope, selected the IOU for $5,000, showed it to Bartlett. "This the agreement?"

Bartlett took the paper, smiled. "Yes, the bridging loan. Y'know, it started an amazing cycle. Carter said he hadn't realised how vital a little extra cash could be sometimes. Since then, well, he kept the $5,000 aside especially for that purpose. Made several such loans. So helpful. Especially with some of our newcomers. A few hundred at the right time can make all the difference."

"I presume everyone always paid up on time?"

"Oh, yes. No trouble there. A debt to the church, y'see. That's how it was operated. Through the church. Carter's idea. Never ever had to ask anyone. Always paid right on time."

Except Hugo Benson, reflected Steven, but possibly the church did not know about Hugo Benson—or Gerrard Townsend who had also benefited by the businesslike generosity of Carter Ancell.

They asked about Luke Ancell but he was not a church member, was not known well, and the interview ended.

Peacock looked at his watch. The Mall was closed. They might as well go back to Lower Hutt, leave Hugo Benson and Gerrard Townsend till tomorrow. They checked in at the office to collect any items of news. Little enough.

A stack of photographs showing the murder scene, before and after the body was removed. All angles. Close-ups. Long shots. Specific areas—the long bench, the safe interior. Pictures of the small office, of the laden shelves in the shop. So many had to be taken because it was not possible to guess which might be the vital one—if any.

A note from Dr Whittaker's assistant to advise the Ancell case had been passed on to him because the doctor had to leave for the Science Congress being held in Auckland. Enclosed was an interim report confirming everything David Galt had already told them. Carter Ancell had taken up to an hour, an hour and a half to die, had died between eleven and midnight. Cerebral haemorrhage. Skull fractured in two places—crushed by a round flat object.

There was no response to the message broadcast every hour on the hour asking Luke Ancell or anyone knowing his whereabouts to contact the police. Still, as Peacock said, early days. There was always tomorrow. If Luke still did not answer time enough then to take some more positive action.

Steven elected to call it a day. He left Jonas brooding over the interim medical report, collected his own car and drove home.

CHAPTER IV

"HOW DOES IT LOOK?" asked Kylie.

"Routine," said Steven. "On the face of it. Present theory—domestic with an attempt to cover by fake burglary."

After all, 90 per cent of all homicides could be classed as domestic. The victim had to know his attacker, therefore it was simply a matter of weeding out possibles until the probable was found.

In this case, Luke Ancell. If—when—he was located, he needed to have a good story to stop police thinking of him as the one most likely to benefit.

After the evening meal, Steven went into the front room to read the evening paper. Kylie stayed in the kitchen, preparing generally for the next day. The doorbell rang. Dimly Steven heard Kylie open the door, the murmur of voices, was not surprised when she looked in smiling.

"You have a visitor," she said brightly.

Steven was flabbergasted when Detective Constable Tai Bennett walked into the room. He jumped up, immediately alert. "Something come up, Tai? Why didn't they ring? Save your time. My time."

Tai shook his head, waved a deprecatory hand. "No. No. This is entirely unofficial. Between-you-and-me stuff. D'you mind?"

"Of course not." Steven frowned slightly wondering what Tai meant. It had to be something serious. Tai's dark eyes were clouded, his usually cheerful face solemn and downcast. "Come on in. Take the weight off your feet."

Quickly he folded the newspaper, indicated a seat by the small magazine table, sat down opposite.

Kylie hovered uncertainly by the door. "Is this man to man talk or can anyone join in?"

Tai smiled bleakly. "Not exactly private, Kylie. It's just—" He stopped, shrugged, sat down slowly in the padded chair.

"Well," said Kylie. "You won't mind if I leave you to it then. I am rather busy right now. One thing or another."

With that she withdrew, closed the door behind her. Steven looked at Tai. "Something on your mind, fella?" he said gently. "Cough it up. Maybe we can work out something between us."

Now that Tai had Steven's full attention he seemed reluctant to begin. He sat hunched and withdrawn, knees wide apart, rubbing his hands together in seeming embarrassment. His eyes flickered from the carpet to Steven, back to the carpet again, finely-chiselled mouth tightening, relaxing, tightening.

Steven watched the brooding face, wondered what could have brought Tai to him. There were others on the force closer, others who shared more in his daily life outside work hours.

At last Tai spoke. "This Ancell thing," he said slowly. "Looks funny to me. Got all the earmarks of the Cheapskate."

"The Cheapskate?"

"Yeh. A cat who's been hitting small knick-knack shops all over the lower part of the North Island. Takes only the cheaper lines. Guess he knows the real stuff's easy to identify but fashion jewellery—" He shrugged.

Steven considered. Tai would know. He was serving his stint with the break squad under Detective Sergeant Rex Wiseman right now. But what had this Cheapskate to do with this unexpected visit?

"You haven't come here to discuss the Ancell case," he said crisply.

"No, I haven't." Tai sighed, looked around the room with desperate eyes. "Maybe I shouldn't have come—busting in on your free time like this. But I didn't want it to be too official, if you know what I mean. And you—you are the man who knows."

"I am?" echoed Steven in surprise. "Depends on what you're talking about. Are you in some kind of trouble, Tai?"

Tai shook his head, pulled a face. "Not me. It's just—" He sighed again, leaned back, looked squarely at Steven. "It's this inquest thing. At Nelson. I had a visitor tonight. About an hour ago. Maui Puhanga."

"The city councillor?"

"Yes. Seems the Pykes are cousins six times removed or something. You know what it's like. Blood ties and everything. Then I'm police so he came to me. Y'know. Looking-after-your-own sort of thing. I could've read your report, I guess but, well, I don't think I should discuss information obtained from official files with out-

siders. I thought—I thought if you talked to me about it—unofficially—it would be okay to pass it on."

The brown eyes were pleading for understanding.

Steven smiled to himself. Poor old Tai. Trying so hard not to put
a wrong foot forward in his probationary years. He remembered
how delicately he himself had trodden the probationary path so he
could understand why Tai was being so careful but in this case . . .

"Sure I can talk to you, Tai. Unofficially. After all it was a public
hearing. No stay on information. But Asa Pyke was at the hearing
—with his legal beagles. They must've given him a full transcript.
Otherwise he was wasting his money."

"That side of it's all right, I guess. But Maui thinks Pyke wasn't
entirely satisfied. A feeling he had or something. And he doesn't
know what he can do about it. Anything or nothing. So if you talk
to me about it—unofficially—maybe we can spot something that
doesn't sit right."

"Maybe," said Steven thoughtfully. Inwardly he was not hopeful.
It was a matter of blood ties. Asa Pyke felt something simply
because the deceased had been his son. The premonitions of the
next of kin. The unexplained fears of a parent. There were hundreds
of stories to substantiate such things. Neither Steven nor Tai had
that closeness. They were onlookers, seeing, hearing but not feeling.

Steven kept his thoughts to himself in the face of Tai's earnest-
ness, launched into a detailed account of the inquest from the
moment he sat down in that row of witnesses to the time the coroner
gave his finding.

When he finished he waited for Tai's comment, was not surprised when the big man shrugged his shoulders, smoothed a pensive
hand across his mouth.

"Yes, that's more or less what I expected. But Maui seemed to
be implying that Cody was really murdered. Worse—that police
were covering up for some reason or other."

Steven spoke sharply. "The person who did all the covering up
was Asa Pyke. He was so anxious to keep his son's name clean
he—or rather his legal reps—bulldozed the court into accepting
the fact that the person I'd seen abducted or whatever was not his
son. And if that person wasn't Cody, then the accident verdict was
a foregone conclusion."

He watched Tai closely but the other returned his gaze unblink-
ingly. "You understand? It just happened Cody was dressed in
that outfit. It just happened he climbed into the chip pile. All these

43

things just happened. No connection. Asa Pyke made sure of that. Now he's having second thoughts, is he?"

"So it seems. What d'you think, Steven? D'you think he could've been murdered?"

Steven stiffened. He thought back to Peacock's caustic demand for his opinion, his own reply.

"I have to accept the court's findings," he said levelly. "The men who did the actual investigation seemed satisfied. They knew all the facts. I didn't. Who am I to disagree?"

Apparently it was the wrong thing to say.

Tai smiled coldly. "Yeh, I get the picture. Well, thanks anyway. I'll let Maui know they just gotta accept things the way they are. Not that they expected anything different, I guess."

He stood up, face hard, lips tight, eyes carefully not looking at Steven. "Sorry to have bothered you, Sergeant," he said curtly.

Steven jumped up, stepped in front of the disgruntled Tai. "Stop right there, Constable!" he said harshly. "You're not going anywhere. Not just yet. You're going to listen to me. And listen good! Up to this moment everything we've discussed can be considered unofficial. You can tell your friends anything you like about that. But from now on—if you breathe a word of what we're going to talk about to anyone—anyone at all—I'll turn you inside out and hang you out to dry. Now, sit down and stop being such a damn fool!"

Tai flinched, sat down reluctantly. Steven surveyed him with as stern a countenance as he could manage.

"Right. Now, let's get this straight. What happens now is strictly between you and me. Official. Stamped 'for your eyes only'. That sort of thing. You are police—and don't you ever forget it. Police. Just now you suggested the coroner's finding was incorrect. So what are *you* going to do about it?"

"Me? I—I—" Tai floundered, bewildered by the turn of events.

"Yes, you! You're the one in a position to do something. Not your friends. They can snarl as much as they like but they were so clever they cut the ground from under their own feet."

Tai continued to gaze blankly at him.

"Don't you see? They can't claim Cody was murdered unless they admit he was the one in the car park. And they won't do that. You can bet on it. But you—you're police. You're supposed to be objective. You stand on the sidelines. If you see something that doesn't seem right, you're supposed to do something about it. Without fear or favour. Remember. So what d'you propose to do?"

44

"Do? There's nothing—I mean the coroner said—"

Steven shook his head impatiently. "So what. The coroner's findings can be put aside. You know that. That's been the law ever since the Elsie Walker case."

He sat back to watch Tai, letting that vital fact sink in, noting doubt, elation, chase each other across the mobile face.

The Elsie Walker case. The coroner's finding in that case was death from exposure but subsequent events linked her death with one of the most gruesome murders in New Zealand history, suggesting that she, too, might have been murdered. After that, the law was amended to allow a coroner's finding to be set aside if sufficient evidence could be produced to prove that finding incorrect.

"You mean—we can re-open the case just like that?"

"Not quite. It won't be easy. We have to show good reason. Proof. What proof have you, Tai, besides idle chatter?"

"I don't know. I haven't thought about it much."

"No, you haven't. You haven't thought about it at all. You've allowed yourself to be conned into thinking along emotional lines instead of reasoning things out."

Steven suddenly dropped his reproving tone, became more amenable. "All right. Let's start again. Look at the case objectively. The same as any other case."

Tai grimaced, instantly alive and alert. "That fellow in the car park. It could've been Cody Pyke!"

"I always believed that. But I can't prove it. No way."

"But suppose it was. D'you think he could've been killed right there? While you were watching?"

"What makes you say that?"

"Well, you said another guy came up behind him, then Cody began to struggle."

"Okay. Now explain the pathologist's evidence. Fragments of beechwood fibre in the lungs. Remember?"

"So they drugged him, carted him to the chip pile, left him there to suffocate."

"No sign of drugs in the body. Other than a small dose of alcohol. Not enough to make him drunk even."

"All right. They made him unconscious some other way. Like a bit of pressure on the right nerve. That could do it."

"They carted him from the Rutherford car park on one side of Nelson right over to the chip pile out at the port. Had to keep him quiet all that time."

"But there were three guys. One to drive. The other two in the back holding him down perhaps. You did say bruises on his arms."

"Slight bruising only. No deep bruises or signs of restraint."

Tai shook his head in exasperation. "Crazy, isn't it? No marks on the body so he went of his own accord. We say, kidnapped. Chap says it'd take a long time to suffocate. So he had to be dead when he was thrown on the chip pile. Yet he breathed in wood fibre—fibre identical with the beech chips stacked there. Proves he wasn't dead. He was still alive? Yet he just sat there and suffocated. Why weren't there marks on his hands and arms to show he tried to fight his way out? All right, so he wasn't dead. Just unconscious maybe. But how? Doesn't make sense!"

"No. It doesn't make sense. Of course, there is the possibility that the man in the car park was someone else entirely."

"Who, for instance?"

Steven shrugged. "We—ell, an accomplice. Maybe someone Cody had teamed up with to rip off the Rutherford. Only these others interfered. Members of another gang perhaps."

"So when his cobber failed to show, Cody drifted off, went down to the chip pile with a couple of bottles and—" Tai's lips curled. "Don't like that one little bit."

"No. But it is logical. Fits the facts. After all, if I hadn't glanced out of the window at that particular moment, no one would've known about the car park bit."

"Yeh—and Asa Pyke's law boys took care of that, didn't they. So what's left? Only the fact that Cody was found suffocated in the chip pile. The extra bits and pieces don't mean anything in that context."

Steven watched Tai quietly for a moment. "D'you still think murder? Remember—every sudden death isn't necessarily murder."

Tai hesitated. "I don't know. I really don't know. On the face of it, an accident. Yes. For sure. But I've got a feeling about this one. Won't be happy till I've got it out of my system."

Steven nodded. "Fair enough. And I'm with you. So we take another look, eh? Privately. Soon as we produce some evidence, we'll talk to the powers-that-be. You'll have to do all the legwork, though. Won't be difficult. You're in a good position. Maui approached you. Be expecting you to ask questions."

"Questions? What sort of questions? It happened in Nelson."

"So it did. But the Nelson angle's been thoroughly investigated. I myself had a mooch around the car park next morning. Being in the business, so to speak. Didn't find anything interesting. Whole area singularly clean and tidy. A little debris caught amongst the bushes at the side. Cigarette packets, bits of paper—what you'd expect. Nothing sinister. You can bet the local boys gave it more than a once-over, too. And the chip pile. By the time the scene squad arrived that area was well trodden over. Surface chips spaded away. Remember? No. Nelson's out. Your—our best bet is right here. Cody's associates. They might know something. Find out where that outfit came from, could be it will point a finger."

"Maybe his father will be willing to talk now?"

"Wanna bet? Besides, he probably doesn't know anything. Says himself Cody never talked to him."

He shook his head. "No, Asa Pyke's out. But Cody's friends. That's different. Cody was being secretive about this Nelson trip— yeh—but there's a chance he did let something slip. Something we can build on." He paused. "What was he like anyway?"

"Cody?" Tai frowned. "Didn't know him myself. Maui says he was stupid rather than bad. Sort of guy who'll do anything to try to impress his cobbers. No more brains than a chicken."

"But his people are decent people. That's why Maui's concerned. Why you want to get stuck into it."

"I feel I owe them. Something I have to do."

"Right. As for me—well, there are too many loose ends. Too many questions unanswered. Goes against the grain." He stopped, considering, spoke slowly. "For your information, there are one or two things that didn't come out at the inquest. Item one—Cody Pyke was booked in at his hotel under a false name. That's why the body wasn't identified till the Wednesday. They went haring off after the person named in the hotel register."

"Well, well! So Cody was up to something."

"Seems like. Although his people don't need to know that bit. Item two—you know my evidence. I said I saw this slighter man come up behind the one in hotel uniform, put his hands on his shoulders. That's exactly what I saw. But he didn't put his hands on the chap's shoulders immediately. He sort of lifted them above the guy's head. Then put them on his shoulders. Y'know what I thought? I thought he was slipping a noose around that fella's throat."

He grimaced. "That's why I went for the phone. So you can imagine how I reacted when they said there were no marks of violence on the body. I mean, there's no way you can hide a garrotting. No way!"

"You believe it's murder, too, don't you?" said Tai accusingly.

"Very possibly it is murder. But how? When? Nothing fits. All

47

the pathological evidence is at variance with what I saw. What I thought I saw. My own conclusions. Which means we are walking on air. We've got nothing. So go carefully. Talk to Maui. Talk to Cody's friends. As I said, they'll be expecting questions to a certain extent. But don't be too insistent. You don't want to sound too curious. Not yet."

Tai nodded. "I'll play it low key. Routine inquiry. Y'know. Tell them every sudden death isn't necessarily murder—even an odd one like this. I'll point out the medical report did emphasise no signs of violence. Agree with Asa Pyke the chap seen at the car park was someone else entirely. That should cool things."

Steven smiled thinly. That was certainly magnanimous of Tai in view of his earlier hostility. "Anything else, Tai?"

"Yes. How come that bit about the false name and so on was not brought out at the inquest?"

"Question wasn't asked. Besides it wouldn't have altered anything. Why volunteer something so absolutely irrelevant?"

Tai chuckled. "Yes. That's right. Answer the question you're asked. Nothing more. Elementary instructions."

He stood up, stretching his legs slightly.

"Well, thanks, Sarge. That's certainly cleared the air a lot—with me, anyway. I'll let you know when I turn up something. If I turn up something."

"Well, don't forget," said Steven, coming to his feet to escort Tai to the door. "Keep this all under your cap. I'm the only one you're to discuss it with. Okay? Time enough when we've got something concrete to go on. Then we can start stirring. And I mean stirring. Meantime you don't know anything. Okay?"

"I dig. And believe me—is that a load off my mind." Tai waved a cheery goodbye as Steven closed the door, perfectly happy now he had shared his doubts without having to take an official stand.

"Well, what was that all about?" asked Kylie folding a teatowel.

"I don't know exactly. Seems I've volunteered to wet-nurse a DC." Steven laughed softly. "Tai got himself all tied up over some rumours. Wanted to know procedure. Mightn't be anything in it, but we're giving it a go. Together. So you'll be seeing quite a bit of Tai from now on. He's reporting to me every night—till we've got something definite to work on."

Kylie said nothing. She knew when not to ask questions. Steven would tell her when he was ready.

CHAPTER V

WEDNESDAY MORNING. As soon as Steven had skimmed through the daily crime reports he went to the break squad to ask a few questions about burglars.

He found Detective Sergeant Rex Wiseman in a happy mood. "You look as though you've won the lottery," said Steven. "How come?"

Wiseman grinned broadly. "We got the Ghoul last night. Been laying for him for months."

"At Ancell's? We left Mat Ruakere there last night in case."

Wiseman frowned his puzzlement, shook his head. "No. Woman named Cameron. Funeral notice in the paper last night. One of two places we staked out. Decided that was the way this slob worked. Y'know, watching the papers, marking places where deceased lived alone. If he could do it, so could we. It worked."

"Yes. They get away with it for a while. Then they get a mite too clever. Like the one you call the Cheapskate. What can you tell me about him?"

"Oh, him. We've got a lovely big file on him. You're welcome to it." He went to the cabinet, sorted through, plumped a fat file on the desk in front of Steven with an amused grin. "Plenty of information. Adds up to nothing. Covers too wide an area. Y'know. Reports here from all divisions in the lower part of the North Island. Doesn't patronise just us. Probably thinks the territory spread a safeguard."

Steven took the file back to his desk, started ploughing through, taking notes as he went.

As Tai had said, Cheapskate hit any shop selling costume jewellery. Not only knick-knack shops but also watchmakers, chemists, even small department stores.

The most interesting piece of information was that Cheapskate had been operating for over two years. His first attempts were cautious. Country areas. Months apart. Practice runs? Fifteen months ago he moved into the towns, hits becoming bolder, more frequent, although still spread over a wide area.

His total score might never have been realised except that one investigator had been intelligent enough to ask other divisions if they had come across such a burglar. From then on information about Cheapskate was immediately circulated to all divisions concerned, the last recorded hit being at Palmerston North, an inland city a hundred miles to the north of Lower Hutt.

At the bottom of the sheet summarising police co-ordination in this matter were the words: "What does this mean? Someone acquainted with police districts? Procedure? Knows we work mostly within our own boundaries? Do not co-operate as much as we should?" The questions were written in pencil, remained unanswered, noted down before they were forgotten.

Steven read through an analysis of the last ten cases covering a period of six months. No hit amounted to much moneywise but, in all, over $7,000 had been taken. Lines that could not be positively identified. All medium-price-range stuff. Nothing that required a size.

Brooches. Necklaces. Bracelets. No rings. No earrings. No watches—although four hits were watchmaker-jewellers. Nothing that could be proven as coming from a particular shop. Nothing that would be difficult to unload.

Every theft appeared to be by the same person. Over such a wide number of cases little things began to show. No fingerprints. Everything left neat and tidy. Entry professional—various—lock pick, plastic lever, pass key. Burglar alarms bypassed (7). Locked display cabinets broached without damage (6). Locked display cabinets untouched (4), all containing articles of no interest to Cheapskate. Safes opened (5) mostly elderly. Left open. More modern safes untouched.

Steven thought back to the open safe in Ancell's shop. Definitely elderly. There had been other things of value in it, mostly the makings of homecraft jewellery. If Cheapskate had visited Ancell's, surely he would have helped himself to the display on that wall at the back of the shop. The fact that they were still there proved what? That he was interrupted by Ancell's unexpected arrival? That it was simply a cover-up?

By the time Steven had satisfied himself that he knew everything he could learn from the information available, Peacock had arrived. He gave the older man time to read through the crime sheets for the day, showed him his findings.

Peacock grimaced. "Can't ignore it entirely. Better get Mrs Martin to make out her inventory of missing items as soon as possible. Or Luke—when he comes in."

He looked sharply at Steven. "Didn't know about that, did you? We've located Luke. At New Plymouth, so he wouldn't have heard any of the local broadcasts. Travelling for Wright, Benton and Steele. His boss, a Mr Travers, rang about seven, said he'd heard the broadcast, checked in to see what it was all about. We just said we wanted to notify Luke about his uncle's death. Travers said, leave it to him. He'd tell Luke."

"And Luke?"

"Rang Driscoll to say he'd be in to see us about nine or ten this morning. Ringing from New Plymouth, of course." He looked at his watch. "Come on. We'd better get over there. Don't want to keep honest citizen Ancell waiting."

Steven smiled inwardly at the cynicism showing through Peacock's comment. Yet, as a policeman, it was right that he should not accept anything at face value.

Peacock started gathering up the papers he wanted to take with him. "Incidentally, Driscoll also had a ring earlier. A woman. Anonymous. Said Luke was out of town. No use broadcasting. Hung up. No name. Nothing. Youngish voice, Driscoll thought."

"A girl friend?"

"Possibly. He's that age. But she wasn't getting involved, whoever she was." He paused, looked at Steven standing immobile beside his desk. "Something on your mind?" he asked brusquely.

"Nothing to do with the Ancell case," said Steven carefully. Jonas shrugged, gestured impatiently.

Briefly, unofficially, Steven told him about Tai Bennett's visit. Jonas heard him out, nodded. "So you've got yourself a backer, eh? Well, you'd better follow through. But keep it downbeat. Not enough to make Bennett think it's being shelved or anything. You never know—something might even come up. If so, we make it official. But I don't want any stirring just for the sake of stirring. The sooner Bennett realises that the better. He's police now. Thinks police. Acts police. He doesn't favour anybody. Anywhere. Any time. But—" He heaved himself to his feet. "Bennett must be made to realise all that by himself. The only way he'll get it out of his system." He lifted his eyebrows quizzically. "What d'you think of his chances?"

"Practically nil. But he does have an inside running. More than we do. Maui will talk to him. Asked for an inquiry more or less.

51

If Bennett shows he's doing something about it—even if it comes to nothing—well, it will be a good exercise in public relations, if nothing else."

As they drove over to Wainui, they discussed the Nelson case. Jonas seemed singularly interested in why Asa Pyke had suddenly changed his mind but Steven could not enlighten him.

They arrived at the patrol base a quarter of an hour before Luke kept his appointment, time to discuss the Cheapskate angle. David Galt was frankly sceptical. He admitted there were signs that matched. The right stuff had been stolen. The burglar alarm was the same type bypassed on four other occasions.

The safe had been opened—left open. No prints worth noting. But only the Delacourt consignment had been taken. Nothing else in the shop had been disturbed. That fact still had to be confirmed but it was a fairly safe assessment.

Why did Cheapskate, if it was he, open the safe when he could have helped himself to the items on the display wall, more easily, more profitably. David leaned more to the theory that the safe had been opened by someone who knew where the key was kept, someone who had stolen the Delacourt consignment purely as a cover.

The discussion for and against was interrupted by the arrival of Luke Ancell, whose appearance caused the others to remember errands still to be run.

Steven's eyes opened wide when the young man was ushered in by Driscoll. No one, but no one, had prepared him for Luke Ancell.

Thick blue-black hair, a trifle long, waving fully from the high forehead. Eyes startlingly blue against the tanned skin. Features perfect—straight nose, straight eyebrows, full lips, rounded chin. Short perhaps, around five-six, but good shoulders, narrow hips, muscular legs.

He was wearing a honey-beige overshirt, short-sleeved, open-necked; cinnamon brown shorts; sandals. Around his neck a thick silver chain with a Gemini medallion pendant. On his left wrist, a silver watch, slim, elegant.

Luke Ancell. Prime suspect. Sole heir to Carter Ancell. He spoke in a pleasant baritone when he acknowledged Peacock's greeting, sat down in the chair indicated, waited, obviously nervous.

Steven listened to the preliminary sparring, watched the light beading of perspiration forming on Luke's upper lip. Well, it was hot in the patrol base but not that hot.

"You've had the situation explained to you, Mr Ancell?"

52

"Yes. Mr Driscoll told me everything. Everything he was allowed to tell me, that is. D'you know—who—why—"

"Not yet. No doubt you heard the newscast saying items of fashion jewellery are missing?"

"Yes." Wearily. "That means a burglar, doesn't it? Though why he had to kill Uncle Car—"

"It could've been a cover-up," interrupted Peacock smoothly.

"A cover-up? You mean—like someone took the stuff to make out it was a burglar!"

"It's been done before. Usually by someone who has something to gain by the victim's death. Setting the scene to make it look like an intruder. So as soon as you let us know exactly when you left for New Plymouth—"

"Me? You think—but I—I wouldn't hurt Uncle Car."

"You did quarrel with him though. Loud enough and often enough for others to notice."

"Yes, but that was just—well, it was just a clash of personalities. Uncle Car thought he owned me. Tried to run my life. And I objected."

"You've worked with Carter Ancell five years, they tell me. Was last month any different?"

Peacock waited but Luke simply shook his head in negation. "All right. Suppose you tell us about your New Plymouth trip. Mr Travers said you left yesterday morning."

A wary look came into Luke's eyes. "No. I was supposed to go up yesterday morning but actually I went Monday night. Nine or nine-thirty. To get an early start."

"I see. So you arrived at New Plymouth at—?"

"Well, not till Tuesday morning around eight. I—I stopped at the side of the road. Dossed down in the car. Slept a bit later than I meant to, actually."

"And then?"

"Then I booked into the motel, had breakfast—a tidy up—and started on my calls."

"At what time?"

"I don't know exactly. Around mid-morning, I guess. A bit later than usual but, like I said, I—er—overslept."

"So you said. Now, Mr Ancell, perhaps you can tell us some names. Maybe someone will remember. As you must realise, we have to check everyone's statement. So we need the name of the motel, at least two of the firms you called on and, also, exactly where you parked the car for this sleep you had."

Luke seemed a trifle uneasy but he answered readily enough, named the motel, buyers at two firms, the location of his overnight stop south of Virginia Lake on the edge of Wanganui, waited quietly for the next question.

"When did you first hear about your uncle's death?"

"We-ell, I saw that bit in the paper. The New Plymouth paper. About someone being killed but—" he swallowed. "No name was mentioned so I didn't realise it was Uncle Car. Not then. But later, when I rang my supervisor, Mr Travers—I'm still a new chum so I have to report in each night, discuss progress with difficult clients. So on. Anyway, I rang Mr Travers and he told me about—about Uncle Car. He also told me the police wanted to talk to me. Advised me to come straight back. That's why I rang Mr Driscoll. Told him I'd be in to see you first thing."

Peacock nodded. "Now, Mr Ancell, we want to discuss your relationship with your uncle. You worked with him for five years?"

Luke stirred resentfully. "Yes. I worked for him for five years. Right up till three weeks ago. Then I quit. Got this job at Wright's. Always wanted to travel around."

"You quit. And you weren't exactly friends when you left, were you? You had this quarrel. What was it about?"

"I explained—" He stopped, noting Peacock's granite face, realised there was no escape. "It was nothing much. Just an old man interfering in a young man's life. Y'know. Calling the shots because he looked on me as a son. At least, that's what he said at the time. Didn't stop him from blasting me to hell and back for all that."

"Nothing much, you say. But sufficient for you to tell him he could keep his job—and everything that went with it. Such as a tidy inheritance perhaps." Luke stiffened but remained silent. "You *are* his only kin?"

"Yes. I'm his only kin. My folks were killed a couple of years ago and then he really took over. Oh, he meant well, I guess. Did a lot for me one way or another but—well, I'm not exactly a kid, y'know. I'm grown. Full grown. A man. He kinda kept forgetting that. Set in his ways. Y'know—the shop—church. And me!"

He laughed bitterly. "Not the me I wanted to be. The me he wanted me to be. All right in the beginning. I guess I played along. Pleased the old man no end. But he couldn't leave it at that. Wanted me to change. Be more like him. Pillar of the church. Watching every penny. Every word. Every action. Not because he thought it best for me, y'understand. Because of what other people might think. Preached to me about upholding my place in the community and what-have-you. He forgot I had enough of my father in me to hit back—"

He bit his lip, gave a shaky laugh. "There I go again. I promised —myself I'd keep my trap shut. Only speak when I'm spoken to like. But I have to shoot my mouth off. Can't seem to help it."

He leaned forward soberly.

"I didn't kill Uncle Car, Inspector. I was fond of the old man. He was something special. I know I called him an interfering old busybody when I had my dander up. I know I had a fight with him—several fights—but I also know he thought he was doing what was best for me. What *he* thought was best for me. It did get on my wick sometimes but, deep down, I knew he was on my side. It's just—it's just—he wouldn't leave me alone. He wanted me perfect. His way."

Ruefully, Luke spread his hands. "I had to show him I could manage without him. I thought once I got that across we could join up again. He wouldn't be so hard on me. Y'know."

"I know," said Peacock sympathetically. "It might've worked, too. Only your uncle was killed—and you, I imagine, you inherit."

"I guess so. Uncle Car was very much a family man. And I guess he always knew I'd come around eventually."

"How much d'you think Carter Ancell was worth?"

"No idea. He wasn't rich but I guess he was reasonably well-off. Well, everyone seemed to think so even if he did live like a miser."

"You mean not splashing out on risky expansion and so on?"

Luke started, relaxed. "Yes, that sort of thing. Someone told you, eh? Yes, I tried to talk him into a bigger shop. But Uncle Car didn't think it was the right time."

"Was that what the final quarrel was about?"

"No-o. Of course, we had a slanging match over that one, too, but—no, it wasn't that. That was just business. And I was no match for him there." He toyed absently with the medallion.

"So—what was the quarrel about?" Peacock persisted.

Luke looked up sharply. "Like I told you. He wanted to run my life. I objected. I've got a right to live my own life any way I want. Without any—without any—" He stopped, fingers covering his betraying lips. "Oh, God! If I'd known this was going to happen, I'd have done anything he asked. Anything!" He rubbed the back of his hand roughly against wet eyelashes.

"Sorry about that. Guess it only just hit me. Uncle Car—" He lowered his eyes, left hand swinging the medallion back and forth, back and forth.

"That's all right," said Peacock gently. "A natural reaction. However, there are one or two questions we have to ask. Then you can go. First—when was the last time you saw your uncle?"

"When I quit. Three weeks ago. 19th January to be exact."

"I see. Now, have you ever heard of a burglar who makes a specialty of stealing fashion jewellery?"

"Well, yes. We all knew about him. In the trade, I mean. D'you think he's the one?"

"There were such items stolen. Mrs Martin is going to check on it for us today." Luke made no comment. "Another question. Last night a woman rang to tell us you were out of town. Any ideas?"

Luke shook his head casually. "No. No idea."

"You have a girl friend?"

"No one in particular. Say, you don't expect me to reel off the names of all the females I know, do you?"

"No. That won't be necessary."

"So I can go now?" When Peacock nodded, he still hesitated. "I guess you want me to stick around. But would it be all right for me to go into Wellington and the Hutt this afternoon? I need to contact some of our suppliers. Sort things out with them. About the shop, y'know."

He stood up, ready to leave.

"And I have to see Mr Travers as well. I'm quitting Wright's of course. Won't be much use to them if I can't go travelling. But I owe Uncle Car that much. I mean, someone has to take over. Even if the shop has to—to be sold in the end, it's better if it's a going concern."

"As long as you're available if we need you," Peacock said. "We'll be finished with the shop as soon as Mrs Martin finalises the list of missing items."

When the door closed behind Luke, Peacock looked at Steven. "Well, they were right. Only a boy for all his twenty-four years. Really naïve. I wonder why he's lying. What he's lying about. Well, so much for Luke. Our next job is clearing up this loan business."

They left the patrol base, walked over to the Mall. As they approached, a car stopped by the western entrance. Teresa Martin descended to be met by DC Tai Bennett who escorted her through the swing door in the glass wall. As Peacock and Steven entered Bennett was opening the door of Ancell's Gifts and Novelties, ushering Mrs Martin inside to make up her list of missing items.

It was business as usual in the Mall. Here and there a grey head, the occasional male, but mostly the thin crowd was composed of brightly-clad young women, pushing prams, urging along toddlers, moving from shop to shop with that familiar look of determined purpose. Almost opposite Ancell's was a small group of middle-aged women watching the closed door, whispering together, the only ones seemingly still interested.

The two police officers walked quickly through the crowd.

They turned the corner into the corridor where the manager's office was situated, found Townsend only too happy to answer their questions. He nodded slightly at the mention of the loan.

"A good man. That's what I meant, Inspector. Carter Ancell offered me that loan just when I was feeling quite desperate. You know what it's like. Shifting from one town to another. You have to get somewhere to live down here before you've properly unloaded where you lived up there. That's what happened to me. Money all tied up with the lawyers handling my house sale—and me, trying to buy something suitable down here. I found an ideal place—but was a couple of thousand short of the ready. I could get a bank loan but I needed a guarantor. I asked Carter and he wiped the whole deal. Said he'd advance the money to tide me over. No interest. No lawyer's fees. I tell you I jumped at it. That's the kind of man he was, Inspector. Helpful. Trusting. All I had to do was sign an IOU. Fantastic! Not exactly businesslike but somehow it made me want to prove his faith in me was not displaced. Paid him back as soon as the money arrived from the sale of my Masterton house. Carter told me it wasn't necessary. Didn't want me to be out of pocket. I showed him the cheque so he knew I wasn't exactly depriving myself."

On the other hand, Benson turned sullen when the subject of the loan was raised. "Strictly between Carter and me," he mumbled. "Said I wasn't to tell anyone. Took it for granted he wouldn't talk either."

"But you did sign an IOU, Mr Benson. And of course we found that when we searched his house."

"Oh!" Benson seemed surprised. He scowled, nibbled at a piece of loose skin on his finger, glared at Peacock from under frowning brows. "So you know it's overdue!"

"We know it's overdue," said Peacock mildly. "Maybe you could explain why it's overdue."

"I'm not obliged to," snapped Benson.

"You're not obliged to," Peacock agreed. "But I would point out you were overheard having an argument with Carter Ancell. Only last week. Was it about this overdue loan?" Benson remained silent. "Would it interest you to know that of all the loans Carter Ancell made in this manner, you were the first one to let him down?"

Benson's eyes widened. "You mean the old fool lent other people money on a stupid IOU! Wouldn't stand up in court, y'know. He deserved to lose the lot."

"Perhaps. But no doubt Carter Ancell didn't believe it would ever reach that stage. Not with a friend."

A dull red stained Benson's jowls. He said gruffly, "It was an oversight. That's all! I tried to explain but he wouldn't listen. Got all pious about it. Started preaching at me. Preaching, by God! The more he preached the more I shouted at him. That's what the row was about. Him—preaching. Me—trying to get him to listen. In the end he said we'd better both forget about it for a week or two. Have another talk when I was more rational."

Benson was bitterly angry again. "More rational! I was staggered. Didn't know what to say. Just then Sheila walked in so we kinda let it ride."

As they walked back to the base, they talked about Benson. He had claimed he was baby-sitting on Monday night. Not much of an alibi. Two sleeping children. He could have slipped out easily for, say, half an hour. Could even have arranged to meet Ancell at the shop after the meeting. If so, surely he would have made some attempt to recover the IOU—yet the house keys had been discarded almost immediately and Ruakere had reported an undisturbed night.

Steven found on the desk a report of the accident in which Luke's parents were killed. All too familiar—too much drink, too much speed—and a list of the contents of the safe.

On the bottom: two rolls of copper wire, one of silver; four sheets of 16g copper 14″ × 12″, one sheet of silver 9″ × 6″; three partitioned boxes, one containing jeweller's findings (hinges, pins, earscrews, catches, etc.), two containing gemstones, pieces of ivory, etc., for mounting; flat steel block of polished steel, 3″ × 3″ × 1″.

First shelf up: cheque book, part-used; cash book; three sales docket books, one in use; receipt book; ledger.

Second shelf up: three order books, one in use; box file of outstanding orders; inward shipping file; bank statement file.

Top shelf: two hand-made necklaces, dropped pendant style on silver chain, both featuring oval pottery pieces set on silver surround.

At ten to twelve, Mrs Martin rang to say she had the list ready.

CHAPTER VI

STEVEN WENT BACK to the Mall. Tai Bennett was waiting to open the door of Ancell's Gifts and Novelties. He led the way to the office at the back of the shop where Mrs Martin was putting away papers she had been using for her check.

A tiny office, room only for a kneehole desk in the right corner, a narrow bench on the wall abutting the shop, a wall whose top half was one-way mirror glass so that an assistant could work at the bench, watch the shop at the same time.

Teresa Martin seemed completely recovered from her experience of the day before. Her motherly face showed a certain sadness but she smiled briefly at Steven, said quietly, "It wasn't much of a job after all. Only the stuff from Delacourt's has been taken."

She handed Steven copies of the packing-slips/invoices. "Y'see, Mr Ancell has ticked off the items received. He always did that. As soon as anything arrived. Then he'd put them into the safe until they were priced and put into shop stock."

Attached to the two packing-slips/invoices was a copy of the order from Ancell's against Delacourt & Son, manufacturers of high-quality costume jewellery, New Zealand souvenirs, paua-shell and greenstone jewellery. Each paper was ticked, counter-ticked. One item on the order had the quantity ringed, another figure written in beside it. The quantity ordered was four, the figure written in three.

"Anything special about these?" asked Steven.

"No. The usual type of thing. Pretty-pretty. Not too pricey."

Steven looked at the total at the bottom of the second page—$375 as David Galt had said.

"Any idea when this stuff arrived, Mrs Martin?"

"No. But it must've been fairly late. I work till four. So it must've been after that."

"Can you show me a Delacourt item?"

"Well, yes. This is a Delacourt necklace." She lifted the decorous

59

chain she was wearing. Made of alternate lengths of flat gold with here and there oblong bubbles fashioned from gold thread, it gleamed softly against the sheen of her dress. A double strand which probably meant two separate necklaces, the twin looping being more decorative than a single string.

"Very pretty," said Steven. "Are they all that type? No jewel insets or anything?"

Mrs Martin smiled. "Well, it's the fashion trend right now. Gold on gold. Silver on silver. But they do insets in some pieces. Not real jewels, of course. Imitation or low-priced gemstones. I'll show you."

She let Steven into the shop, pointed out three separate items on the display wall. A brooch made of flat gold wire twisted to hold a brown goldstone, cabochon-cut; a deep-blue emerald-cut pendant on a silver chain; a striped tiger's eye peg-set in a silver ring.

Steven asked about other pieces on the wall. All attractive, modestly priced. Fully one third were Delacourt productions. More than half were the types favoured by Cheapskate.

Under the display counter holding more expensive pieces were small boxes, yellow, white, blue and red. "What are those for?" asked Steven.

"Oh, those. When we sell anything we like to put the article into its own box. These are Delacourt boxes." She indicated some white containers, opened one to show the scarlet satin inlay. "That's a brooch box. This one—" She touched another shape. "That's for a ring and that's for a necklace. You soon get used to the different shapes."

She looked at Steven, waiting for his comment. He shook his head, went back into the tiny office, picked up the list she had made out as a translation of the coding on the Delacourt order. It showed 25 items, necklaces, brooches, bracelets.

"Well, thank you very much, Mrs Martin. We've told young Luke he can take over the shop any time he wants."

"Luke? He's back?"

"Yes, he's back," Steven said carefully. "Why back? Did you know he'd been away?"

Mrs Martin flushed. "Not exactly—but well, I know someone at the—flats and she told me—she told me you'd been around. And Luke wasn't there." She seemed embarrassed at this display of natural curiosity. "Y'see, I wanted to—to tell him about Mr Ancell. I thought—" She stopped lamely. "I'm just an interfering old busybody at heart, I suppose. That's one thing Luke hated more than anything."

"So I believe," said Steven smoothly. "That's why he quarrelled with Carter Ancell, isn't it?"

Mrs Martin turned away. "Perhaps. Mr Ancell was afraid Luke might turn out a no-good like his father if he didn't keep a tight rein on him. Of course, the tighter you hold a boy in the more likely he's going to rebel."

"You knew Luke's father, Mrs Martin?"

Again the deep pink to the cheeks. "Luke's father was—was a womaniser," she said primly. "I don't know how poor Madeline put up with him. Such a pretty little thing. But so weak. Just put up with everything Luther did. Even though it meant constant heart-break—and struggle. If it hadn't been for Carter Ancell—well, I don't know how they would've managed."

"Was Carter Ancell a womaniser, too, Mrs Martin?"

She gasped. "Sergeant, how could you! Carter Ancell was the nicest, kindest man you could meet. A perfect gentleman. Always courteous. Always gentle."

"I'm sorry if I offended you, Mrs Martin. But you must remember we didn't know Mr Ancell. We can only go by what people tell us. Some people say he was very quarrelsome."

"Outspoken maybe—but definitely not quarrelsome, Sergeant. If he thought something needed to be said, he'd say it. That's all."

"He did quarrel with Luke though."

"Yes. But that was different. That was personal. Something just between the two of them."

"You know what it was about then?" Steven prompted.

But the woman shook her head firmly. Steven had a feeling she was concealing something. To protect Luke? To protect Carter? Benson had implied that any quarrelling between the Ancells had been strictly business. Which meant the quarrel Mrs Martin had overheard had to be something different.

Steven folded the paper carefully, placed it in his pocket. "It looks as though my next job is a visit to Delacourt's. Who is your contact there, Mrs Martin?"

"Why, Mr Delacourt senior. He's the one we deal with."

Steven left the blue depths of the Mall, walked out into the blazing sunshine. He reported back to Jonas who agreed he should talk to Delacourt, made an appointment and immediately after a hurried lunch he turned the car's nose out of the valley along the tree-lined main road towards the hill. There were no more than a dozen cars on the access road that, at peak hours, was choked with traffic—a few delivery trucks coming and going.

Breasting the top of the hill, Steven glanced out over the placid waters of the harbour, stretching silver-blue to the far shores of Wellington. It looked tantalisingly inviting with its array of pleasure boats, thick off the Petone foreshore and around the boat harbour on the other side. Further over, the inter-island ferry was making its turn towards the entrance on the way to the South Island, reminding Steven of his trip to Nelson.

He wondered idly if Tai would make any headway with his inquiry. Or were they simply wasting their time?

At last he was down on the floor of the Hutt Valley, the heat haze undulating with the motion of the car. Yet it was cooler over here, a sea breeze stirring the trees into lethargic motion.

Steven found Delacourt & Son in a back street on the other side of Lower Hutt beyond the bridge spanning the sullenly-flowing river. A concrete and glass building, narrow, three-storied, office and display area occupying the front portion of the ground floor.

Mr Delacourt was small and spare, thin grey hair, deep-set eyes. He took the list of merchandise from Steven, tut-tutting over the reason for his visit. He spoke over the intercom to someone named Percy. "Look up the last order from Ancell's, will you? Check with Charlie when it was delivered. The exact time. And bring me two each of at least six items ordered."

While they waited, Delacourt explained their method of operation. Not exactly assembly-line but highly mechanised nevertheless. Precision engineering in precious metals, someone had called it. It meant they could produce a wider range in greater numbers to meet present demand. Nowadays, they catered mainly for the young who did not insist on the one-off type of thing, were quite happy with pretty baubles that were inexpensive but attractive. He and his son tried out new designs now and then. The ones that proved popular were automatically incorporated in the Delacourt list.

Percy arrived with his dozen pieces which he lay on a backing of black velvet. He also brought the information that Charlie had delivered the consignment at precisely 5.20 p.m. on Monday.

Steven nodded, leaned forward to examine the offering. As Mrs Martin said, they were mostly plain or textured gold worked into fairylike patterns. Only two had "jewels"—agate, citrine.

He picked up two apparently identical necklaces, found ever so slight differences, not enough to identify either piece.

"You supply jewellery shops all over New Zealand?" he asked.

"We also export. Building quite a thriving export business. Australia. The Pacific." He smiled at Steven's surprise. "And for your information, retail outlets aren't just jewellery and gift shops. Many stores carry a fashion jewellery counter now—chemists, department stores, supermarkets. A sideline they've found quite profitable." He looked casually through the glass windows surrounding the office. "Even the odd bod with no shop. Like those fellows."

As he waved his hand outwards, Steven turned to see what he meant. In the next room Percy was conferring over items on display with two men, both about the same height, build, wearing light-weight suits, one silver-grey, the other charcoal with an occasional fleck of red. The back of the fair man seemed familiar to Steven but he did not place him immediately.

He turned back to Delacourt. "And they are?" he asked.

"Company reps. At least, the dark one is. A regular customer. In the cheaper lines, of course. Takes them with him on his trips. Plenty of people in the back country only too pleased to pick up a bargain in Delacourt trinkets. Of course, he wouldn't put on such a high mark-up as a shop."

Steven nodded, looked again into the other room. The fair man had turned so he could see his profile, recognise him as Rob Henshawe, a former police officer. Steven was surprised but it had nothing to do with him. He resumed his conversation with Delacourt, asking him to confirm Mrs Martin's detailed descriptions of the missing pieces. While he was doing this a discreet knock came on the door. Percy entered.

"Excuse me, sir, but we have a new customer who wants you to approve credit."

Delacourt frowned at the interruption. "Well, you know the rules. Two character references and the first order no less than $100. Now—"

Percy hesitated, looked at Steven. "Well, Mr Summerfield is quite happy to vouch for his friend. That's one. But they were wondering if this gentleman here would oblige. I understand he knows Mr Henshawe and it is merely a formality as we are already acquainted." He added for Steven's benefit. "You simply have to affirm he is of good character, that's all."

Steven laughed. "Is that all? Easy. Be only too pleased."

"Come in, gentlemen," said Percy opening the door wider. The two men entered. Rob Henshawe made straight for Steven, clasped his hand heartily.

"Hi, Steven. How goes it? Long time no see. Last place I expected to find you." He grinned companionably but his eyes were wary, waiting for Steven's reaction.

Steven did not need to pretend. He was pleased to see Rob again looking fit and well. "Hi, there, yourself. Good to see you again. How're things with you? All right?"

"Fine! Fine!" replied Rob, the smile a little less, the eyes a little darker. "Taken to this travelling lark like a natural. Ask old Frank here. He'll tell you."

He pulled the other man forward, introduced him as Frank Summerfield—black laughing eyes, engaging grin. He gave Steven a paper, pointing out his own name already in the allotted space. Steven quickly scanned the three-line character reference, signed under the neat, precise signature, handed the paper back.

When Percy had shepherded the other two out of the room Steven sat for a moment thinking about Rob Henshawe. He became aware that Delacourt was watching him with shrewd eyes.

"Mr Henshawe is, I take it, an ex-cop?" the man ventured.

Steven started, wondering how much the two of them had given away. "Yes. That's right. An ex-cop. Some of them can't take it, y'know. Plays havoc with your social life. Shift work. Calls back. Feel you can't call your soul your own sometimes."

Delacourt nodded, apparently accepting the explanation at face value, returned once more to the reason for Steven's visit. There was not much more to discuss. Soon Steven was leaving the building, walking back to the car.

There was no sign of Henshawe or his companion. Steven felt vaguely disappointed.

He drove off thinking about Rob Henshawe. It was odd meeting him after all this time. How long? A year? It had to be nearly a year since he was "asked" to resign. Unfortunate, but necessary. From earliest days of training, police personnel were schooled in what they could do, what they could not do. Occasionally there were slips. Most of these were corrected in private by severe reprimands from a superior.

Rob's lapse had been only too public—during a routine crowd control job that should have been straightforward, without incident. Fortunately two back-up senior officers stepped in smartly, smoothed the resulting turbulence before it had time to affect the rest of the crowd. After that Rob was considered a liability. He was given the option. He walked out of the force, out of their lives.

Steven stopped thinking about Rob as he was passing the premises of a local mortician. A funeral was in progress, street lined with cars, an adjacent car park nearly full. People were forming into groups beyond the hedge enclosing the assembly area, shaking hands, talking in low voices. Steven pulled into a gap further down the street, parked neatly, sat watching the mourners.

Presently a long black car drove into the courtyard, allowed two middle-aged people to descend, drove off again. Steven recognised the tall bowed figure of the man—Asa Pyke. He had his arm around the woman beside him, small, fragile with grey-streaked black hair, sad brown eyes.

The groups broke up, converged on the chief mourners.

For a moment they were hidden from view. Finally a man dressed in a dark suit came through the door of the chapel adjoining the courtyard, advanced on the crowd, rescued the couple, led them gently into the chapel.

Obediently everyone else filed into the white building after them. Cody Pyke's funeral. He was certainly being given a great send-off even if he had died a lonely death.

Steven waited till the oak doors closed again. He climbed out of the car, locked it, walked quietly to the mortuary gate, donning his jacket as he went. He paused, looked into the empty space. No one in sight. He crossed the courtyard, pushed open the door of the chapel, slipped into a rear seat.

The room was almost full. Even the seat he had chosen was occupied by a family group, father, mother, three children. They looked at him inquiringly as he sat down then turned their attention to where a minister in white surplice was sorting through his notes.

The scent of flowers filled the air, flowers stacked against the rise of a low dais to the right of the lectern. On the dais, jutting from the wall, was a waist-high protrusion in carved wood, where the polished rimu coffin sat on runners in front of a curtained alcove.

There were no flowers on the coffin. Instead of the usual casket spray, there was a multi-coloured cloth of some kind, flung carelessly across like a warrior's cloak. It covered the top half where the brass nameplate would be.

Close by, facing the congregation, stood a skinny fair-haired youth, at ease, hands clasped loosely behind him, on guard like a sentinel. He was wearing the black leathers affected by some bikie gangs, black leathers that would no doubt have a gang patch on the back.

He looked uncomfortably hot in his heavy outfit, face flushed, beads of sweat forming on his forehead, matting the damp hair into tight curls over his temples.

He stood perfectly still, head bowed, long fair hair falling in soft waves against the shining black of his leathers. Standing guard by a comrade's coffin. His lowered eyelids flickered every now and then towards the minister.

A sombre hush covered the whole room, the only sound the soft movements of paper in the minister's hand, the quiet sobbing of someone in the front pew.

The minister coughed quietly, looked over the assembly with professional assessment. In a throaty voice he intoned greetings to relatives of the deceased, friends, began extolling the virtues of Cody Te Whenua Pyke.

Steven listened absently, noting the genuinely sorrowful faces of the people around him, the stern countenance of the mortician standing in the corner of the chapel beyond the coffin.

Presently the brief address ended. The minister reshuffled his notes, turned towards the fair-haired youth, made some pre-arranged signal. The youth straightened, lifted his hands above his head, swung round to face the coffin.

His back displayed the gang patch—predominantly white, the words STAR FIVE curved around a five-pointed star.

He stood there motionless, silent for a moment, suddenly leaned forward, picked up the multi-coloured thing from the coffin. He swung around again with military precision, holding the cloth high above his head—like a banner.

It was about two foot square, so heavily embroidered that little of the original material showed. An edging of the *tukutuku* pattern enclosed trade symbols of motorcycles, tumbled one on top of the other into a mazed conglomerate of colour that gleamed like a battle standard.

Fair-hair lowered the banner to shoulder height, began to speak of Cody Pyke, his friend. A good friend from the sound of things. He mentioned the Star Five Club, the journeys they made together, seeking the forgotten places, the hidden places in the depths of the forests. He spoke of wheels, country roads running free, the wind of speed. Finally, he finished by launching into a mess of doggerel that resolved itself into three short stanzas interposed by the refrain, "Star Five. Star Five. We are the Five."

It was hardly top class, probably written by one of the club members, but the solemn presentation in slow hymnal cadence gave it a dignity beyond the meaning of the words.

The black-clad youth ended his performance. In the fashion of a soldier officiating at the funeral of a top statesman, he folded the banner into a neat square, handed it to someone sitting in the left-hand front pew. It was passed along the rows, handled pensively, reverently.

At last it reached the family next to Steven. They crooned over it together then the youngest child handed it to Steven, brown eyes wide and wet.

Steven took the cloth in his hands, amazed at its softness, at the intricate stitching that painted the patterns. He smoothed his hands over the upturned surface in the manner he had seen the others employ, turned, walked over to the right-hand pew to give it to the tall, dark man regarding him with frowning concentration.

He slipped back into his place, watching the emblem make its final journey along the rows until at last it reached the father and mother of the boy who lay in the coffin.

The minister raised his hands in benediction. While the rich voice was reciting the final blessings the curtain over the recess parted, the coffin slid quietly, steadily out of sight. The curtain fell back into place. It was all over.

A long shuddering sigh ran through the gathering. The parents walked solemnly down the aisle, the father clutching the embroidered cloth, arm protectively around his tearful wife.

The rest of the congregation followed slowly, silently. By the time Steven came out of the chapel, most of the people from the front pews were in their cars, ready to leave.

CHAPTER VII

STEVEN STOOD ON the porch, observing the mortician as he fussily closed the doors, noting the faces of the mourners, particularly the fair youth who, now the ceremonies were over, seemed anxious to leave.

The young man went to the car where Asa Pyke and his wife sat, spoke a few words, a mite too cheerfully, Steven thought, then ran to a blue Holden close by, climbed aboard, calling to some other young people who tumbled into the car until it was nearly overloaded. With a smart turn of the key, the engine roared into life, the crowd of younger mourners zoomed away at speed, waving, waving as they went.

Steven strolled back to his car feeling that now he had seen everything. To his surprise he found a black and white transport vehicle parked beside his. Leaning against his own car, an interested spectator, was Sergeant Lance Brendon, Transport. He flicked a small salute at Steven without taking his eyes from the quickly-dwindling crowd.

"Hi, there, Lance," said Steven. "What're you doing here?"

Lance grimaced. "Having a look-see. Spotted a listed car. Wanted to have a gander at the guys hanging around."

"Listed, you say? Which one?"

"Blue Holden just taken off. Cause an accident some day, that fella. Sure to—the way he drives. Name of Guy Dalziel. Know him? Runs with another dope named Pyke. Cody Pyke. Don't see him around."

"Oh, he's around," said Steven grimly. "His funeral."

Lance brought his gaze round to Steven's face with a comic expression of disbelief. "You don't say? How come? An accident?"

"That was the coroner's finding. You must've read about it. The body in the chip pile at Nelson."

"Sure I read about it. Come to think about it—the name was

68

Pyke, wasn't it. Never connected it with this one though. Well, it just goes to show—" He lapsed into silence.

"This sus list of yours," said Steven. "What for exactly?"

Lance shrugged. "Nothing concrete. Yet. Just keep track of. Y'know. All the boys have the list. We just watch—and hope."

"Wonder you didn't pick him up right now. The way he took that corner. Dangerous driving by anybody's book."

"You kidding? At a funeral? They'd be screaming!" he paused. "The funeral? You went?"

Steven nodded, told him about the extra unusual part.

"Weird, eh?" commented Lance. "Heard of that before. Kind of totem thing. Bikie gangs in Auckland—all the rage. Sort of paramilitary thing."

"Ever heard of the Star Five gang—club—what-have-you?"

"Nope. New one on me. Not a local gang anyway. What's the drift, Steven? Bikie gang's hardly your line. Thought this Wainui murder was your territory."

"It is. Came over to check some evidence. Got sidetracked by this show because I was at Pyke's inquest. By the way, I met an old friend, Rob Henshawe. Remember him?"

"Yeh. Got turfed out because he lost his cool at the demo. Travelling now. For Loan and Merc. Meet him sometimes on the road. Stops for a chitchat. Misses you lawboys a bit. Seems like."

Steven sighed. "Yes. Struck me that way, too. Pity about Rob. He learned the hard way. Well, I'd better be weaving. The old man will be wondering where I've got to."

Lance straightened, looked over Steven's head. "See you've got yourself a fire over there. A big one."

Steven swung around to look towards the Wainui hill. Beyond the dark green curve, the blue summer sky was drowned in white smoke, patched here and there with grey.

"Oh, hell!" said Steven. "That just about makes my day." He hurried to his car, slid aboard, turned on the engine. A flick of his hand in farewell to Lance and he pulled out, sent the car down the street towards the far hills.

As he drove up the wide road, he kept an eye on that threatening smoke cloud. He topped the crest, looked across the valley to the north-eastern hills where easily six acres were ablaze. Not far above the houses! At least that meant the firemen could use the reticulated water system, a point in their favour. Steven was too far away to see any of the activity on the fireground but the sound of a siren meant another machine was going into action.

He dropped down into the valley. In minutes he stopped outside the base, dashed inside to find Mat Ruakere calmly typing reports.

"Hello—where is everybody?" he asked.

"Jonas went into Wellington a little while ago. Wonder you didn't pass him on the hill. Could've. Left you a few odd jobs to fill out the rest of your day." Mat was maliciously gleeful as he pointed to the desk Jonas had been using. "The others—out doing their duty like good little boys. House-to-house except for a couple giving Driscoll a hand. Down at the fire. They're evacuating some of the houses. Bit too close, the fireboys reckon."

Steven moved to the window. From here they had a clear view of the portion of the hill where the glowing flames menaced the houses. Evacuation would be a precautionary measure only but to the people concerned it would be a harrowing experience. Flame on the lower part of the hill. That meant the fire had started close to the residential area, had been swept upwards by the hot off-the-land wind. Kids, probably, playing with matches. When would they ever learn?

He went back to the desk. The sunlight streaming through the wide windows was tinged with fireglow, filling the room with sunset. Steven sat down, looked at the items Jonas wanted checked, rechecked, groaned. All those! He would be here till midnight.

He pushed the list away, began to read through house-to-house reports. Most were negative—or merely confirming earlier statements. The houses that could have been of some use faced the main road—were subjected to the constant sound of traffic. Most of the people questioned were watching TV, traffic noises an accepted background they had long since stopped noticing.

On Monday night a car could have stopped anywhere along that strip, taken off again without being seen or heard except by someone walking. So far they had not been able to locate the someone walking.

Steven sighed, picked up the next sheet of paper covering a telephone message from Lower Hutt to say Carter Ancell's lawyer confirmed that, except for a few minor bequests, Luke inherited everything—estimated value $175,000.

Also from Lower Hutt, a request from Forensic for samples of cat and dog hairs to compare with those found on Carter Ancell's clothing and the floor nearby. Another job for house-to-house. Cat hairs would be simple enough. Probably from Ancell's cat. But dog hairs! The lab suggested a long-haired species.

Steven sat staring at the paper for a long time. Dogs were not allowed in the Mall. Any dog hairs had to be brought in— on Ancell's clothing? On his assailant's clothing? Still too early to tell.

Two notes pinned together—one from Driscoll to say that the neighbour at the flats, Mrs Tollings, stated Luke arrived home Wednesday morning around six-thirty. The other covered information from New Plymouth. The people named on the list forwarded had confirmed Luke's presence. The buyers both said Tuesday morning some time, around ten or eleven. The motel quoted arrival time 8.38 Tuesday morning, checked out at 10.05 p.m. after some telephone calls. If Luke had left New Plymouth at ten he should have arrived home at three or four at the latest. He should have.

Steven put the papers aside, began to work doggedly through the list Jonas had left for him. Shortly after five-thirty, Driscoll arrived. He looked around as though surprised to find Steven alone, sat down wearily, face drawn, eyes bereft.

"Trouble?" asked Steven.

"Yeh. Trouble. Hoping some of the boys would still be here."

Steven shook his head. "Left before five. Mat rounded them all up, took them back to LH. Trouble at the fire?"

"Not the fire. Under control now. Another hour maybe then standby. People all back in their houses. No sweat."

"Oh," said Steven. He jumped up, went to the window. The smoke seemed as thick as ever but the flames—well, yes they were practically non-existent. A fitful flare now and then in the absolute centre. Around the edges of the still-alive burn were ragged bands of black where the fire had been completely doused.

"Okay. Not the fire," Steven moved back to his chair. "What then?"

"Child missing. Name Shane Lismore. Six and a half. Missing since around three. Came home from school with a friend. Primers get out at two-thirty in case you didn't know. Stayed home a bit then went off with friend to his place—couple of streets away. Happened before. Routine almost. Unfortunately this time friend's mother was waiting for him to arrive home so she could go out. She sent Shane home. Didn't ring his mother or anything. Done it before. Shane always went straight home. Only this time—well, this time Shane didn't go straight home."

Driscoll sighed. "Would happen. Anyway, at five his mother rang friend, found Shane had left at three. She rang around—other friends—then remembering the fire came down there. I mean— sort of thing attracts small boys. No sign of him there but she spotted me. Told me about it. I took her home, made the routine area search, told her to stick around in case Shane came back. I thought—well, get some of the boys on it."

The telephone rang. Both men reached for it automatically. Steven drew back his hand. "Your phone," he said simply.

Driscoll nodded, lifted the receiver, identified himself. An excited voice at the other end went into action, talked, talked with Driscoll interposing an occasional yes, yes, when? At last he hung up, leaned back, kneading his face with unhappy hands.

"Shane Lismore. Last sighting on the hill in the middle of the burn. Oh, God!"

The caller had been the mother of the two boys responsible for the fire. She told Driscoll the whole story. Shortly after three a youth on a trail-bike had been riding the firebreaks, had seen the two brothers—eight and ten—in the gorse smoking. He left the fire break, went after them, snarled at them, confiscated their matches, went back to his joyriding. He was on the top ridge when he heard the siren. He looked back, saw the fire well below the point where he had seen the brothers, guessed they had other matches. He came down straight away, rounded up the two boys, took them home, explained to their mother.

He did this for his own protection because he knew he must have been seen on the firebreaks, could be blamed for the fire. The mother was angry, locked the boys in their bedroom. A few minutes ago she let them out, began to question them. She soon realised they were upset about something more than starting the fire. Both were crying, sobbing in a scared way, quite out of character.

At last she managed to calm them. They told her Shane Lismore was up on the hill. He had followed them when they first went there. They shooed him away, thought he had gone home. After the big boy had bullied them, they had run down the hill to another place. And the summer-dried gorse and pigfern had caught fire. They had tried to put it out, could not stop it. Frightened, all they wanted to do was to pretend it never happened—only the trail-bike rider had other ideas. They watched the fire from their bedroom, suddenly remembered seeing Shane. He was playing in a cleared area directly above the place where the fire had started. The flames had raced up the hill, over and past the place where they had last seen Shane.

Steven and Driscoll wasted no time. They locked the base, went straight to the fireground. Arriving there, they hardly glanced at the activity up the hill where men were operating relay pumps to force water through hose sections up to the firefront.

They were in too much of a hurry to consult with the Chief Fire Officer controlling everything by Fire Engine 44-1 parked on a conveniently-empty section. He received their news calmly, relaxed now because he knew the fire was under control.

It had been only a minor burn in his opinion. By minor, he meant subdued quickly without having to call in the helicopters and monsoon buckets used when an acre-devouring burn blazed for days. There was still a chance for the boy—if he had not been in the absolute centre of the fire—if he had used his head—if—if—

One ray of hope! The chief pointed towards the right where the flames had virtually disappeared, smoke turning into fragmented patches. In two places, a glimpse of green. Green in the middle of a burn? Impossible!

The chief explained. Gorse and broom were faster-growing than the natives, tending to take over, hogging the northern slopes facing the sun. Natives on the other hand flourished on the cooler southern faces, holding dampness in gullies protected by land contours from the sun's drying heat. Fire consumed the dehydrated growth, skirting such gullies as it would a stretch of water. If Shane had managed to find shelter in either of them— Again if—

The two police officers wanted to check out the fire chief's suggestion themselves. He vetoed this. They were not properly equipped. His men were. He would send in two men from the Bush Fire Force, men specially trained for the specialist job of fighting bush fires. As an extra precaution, an ambulance would be called to be on hand if needed—although the Emergency Tender carried full medical supplies which his men were trained to use.

He assured them it would take only minutes to arrange a search as he was in constant radio communication with the men on the hill.

He lifted the transceiver he held, placed it near his mouth, spoke crisply to the Fire Controller operating at the fire front.

Far up the hill a helmeted figure in white stepped out of the smoke on to the wide area where the fire-edge had been completely subdued. He conferred with another white-clad man carrying on his back the knapsack pump used to jet water on to small spot fires and other hot spots. The controller's hands waved as he pointed to the gully immediately below them, to the one further over on the far side. Together the two men came down the steep slope at a speed Steven knew he himself would never have attempted.

They kept to the blackened fire-edge until they were opposite the first gully, struck out across the fireground, heavy boots driving through the burned scrub with familiar disregard, disappearing, re-appearing as smoke thickened and swirled around them. They seemed to spend an extraordinarily long time in that first gully. The chief listened on his handset, shook his head.

Steven held his eyes glued to the hill. At last, the white-clad men appeared, paused on the edge to reconnoitre their route to the second patch of green on the other side of the burn. The pump-carrier used his jets on a sudden flare of flame and they were off again, ploughing through the brittle fire-trash, sidestepping patches of flame, looking like devil wraiths dancing up there in the smoke. Down into the second gully. They seemed longer this time. Deeper? More overgrown? Steven could feel the tension building inside himself.

Up on the hill the white pall intensified. The touches of green vanished from sight. Steven was aware only of the smell of burning, the sound of flames crackling their losing battlecry.

The chief touched his arm, pointed upwards. The light wind had shifted the wall of smoke, thinned it to a wispy curtain showing the far end of the gully. Two figures in white stood there. The one with the back-pack lifted his hands in a cheery wave, the other held the slight form of a child. They began their downward journey, the first man breaking ground for the one carrying Shane Lismore.

Soon they were crashing through the last stretch of charred scrub, were on the lower slope of untouched green, finally on level ground. Shane was handed over to the men from the Emergency Tender who immediately applied oxygen, checked for injuries.

The Fire Controller, a broad grin on his young, smoke-grimed face, made his report. He admitted they had nearly missed finding the boy. They had followed some slide marks on the downward slope to discover Shane near the bottom, unconscious. Apparently he had caught his foot in one of the trailing lianas lacing the slopes, tumbled down to hit his head on the trunk of a tree fern. As long as the smack on his head was not too serious, they thought he would be all right.

Almost as they finished speaking, the ambulance arrived. The now fully-conscious Shane was transferred. Driscoll climbed in beside the driver to show him where to pick up Mrs Lismore so she could accompany her son on his trip over the hill to the Hutt hospital.

Steven looked at his watch. Six-twenty. Tai Bennett would be coming to talk to him about Cody Pyke some time after eight. If he went home now he might have enough time for a meal, to relax.

"I don't think I'll ever get the smell of smoke out of my nose," Steven complained to Kylie as he came out of the shower, towelling the wetness out of his hair. "Sort of get the taste into your mouth. Can't get rid of it."

"You'll be all right once you get some food into you," Kylie assured him. To his surprise, she was right. He had thought his appetite completely gone but he enjoyed the goulash Kylie gave him. After the meal, he settled down to read the paper, had hardly begun when Tai arrived.

Hastily, Steven refolded the paper, made room on the magazine table. Tai apologised for the meagre amount of information he had brought with him. He was treading lightly, he explained, making only surface inquiries at this stage.

The parents were still reluctant to admit their son was anything but perfect. Otherwise, they were extremely co-operative. They arranged for several of Cody's friends to come to the house, setting aside a room so Tai could ask about Cody's movements during that final week. Only two items seemed to be of any importance.

Cody's young brother, who shared his bedroom, said on Monday night he had walked in to find Cody in front of the mirror holding this yellow outfit against him. Cody had been annoyed at being seen, hastily packed the costume away in a squarish box lying on the bed.

He explained he was going to work nights at a local cabaret. It might, he said, end in a singing engagement. He made his brother promise not to tell anyone, especially their parents, because he wanted to surprise them.

The other informant worked with Cody at the giant General Motors complex at Trentham, close to Upper Hutt. Usually they lunched together in the cafeteria but that Monday Cody went missing. After lunch, the friend went outside to lounge in the sun, saw a car stop down the street. Cody climbed out carrying a squarish box which he later put in his locker. No, Cody did not tell him what was in the box. He did not ask. None of his business. The car—oh, a beat-up jalopy, station-wagon type of thing, pretty old. No. he did not see the driver. Not close enough.

"A squarish box, eh?" said Steven. "Probably the same one his kid brother saw. Was Guy Dalziel there?"

Tai's eyebrows rose. "No. Nobody of that name. Why?"

Steven told him about the strange happenings at the funeral.

"Funny. No one mentioned Guy Dalziel to me. No one mentioned the Star Five either."

"I wonder why," said Steven softly. "Looks like that's your next job, Tai. Find this Dalziel. He can tell you about the Star Five. All I know—it's not a local gang."

"That fits. Seems Cody hasn't been home overlong. Been working up at Kuwarau. With Tasman Pulp and Paper Mill. Went there couple of years ago. Lost his job August or thereabouts. Came back home. If he belonged to a bikie gang, could've been up there."

"Possible. Not many gang complaints there though."

"Well, Tauranga's pretty close. Get their share during the tourist season. But Star Five! Sounds like maybe only five in it. Minor league. Probably only playing at being bikies."

"Yeh. Imitation stuff. Probably the answer. But I'm curious. Why wasn't it mentioned? Why wasn't Guy Dalziel part of your conference? They ask you to help then monitor proceedings."

"Seems like. But don't let us read too much into that. Probably never even occurred to them. Old hat! After all, I did tell them I was trying to find out what Cody was doing, talking about that last week. Not what happened last year. And the fellows there—all local—the ones Cody had been planning to go to Hastings with. Maybe Dalziel wasn't in on that."

"That's a point. But tomorrow, see what this Dalziel has to say. Way things are now, we're getting nowhere fast. But before we drop it, I'd like to know something about the Star Five. About Dalziel. Is he local? Was he working at Kuwarau, too? Did he come back with Cody in August? Bring me that information and we'll decide what to do."

The more Steven thought about it, the more he was beginning to believe they were wasting their time—everybody's time—despite the evidence of a squarish box that might have contained the Rutherford costume, that might have come from the driver of an old beat-up jalopy of unknown make and forgettable appearance.

CHAPTER VIII

PEACOCK WAS NOT impressed when Steven made his report the next morning. "Looks like a fizzer. Beats me why the old man even brought it up. So anxious to cover up one minute—wiped everything against young Cody. Yet now he's got these misgivings. Granted it's odd. But he can't have it both ways. If Cody was such a good boy, why murder?"

"Because Cody wasn't such a good boy? Might even have a record. I know Petone says he's clean but he hasn't lived all his life in Petone."

Steven watched Peacock closely. The brooding eyes narrowed, the heavy brows pulled into a thoughtful frown. Steven knew what he was thinking. Once they asked Records about Cody it was official. So far, the coroner was satisfied it was an accident. Nelson police were happy with that verdict. Cody's people? Well, there were murmurings—speculation. Nothing definite. Easily damp that down with a few pertinent facts in the right direction. Might even be best to contain it right there.

Once it was official it would be out of their hands. Lower Hutt could hardly launch a full-scale inquiry into something that happened outside their own jurisdiction. Steven could imagine Nelson's reaction to that one. South Island might even resent interference by big brother in the North Island. Probably that was behind Peacock's reluctance to approve an official investigation without adequate cause.

"You might be right at that," said Peacock with a sigh. "Maybe Cody does have a record. As of now, we're not interested. Turn up something indictable against this bikie gang you're talking about, maybe we'll move. But don't expect too much. Not all the people who ride motorbikes are anti-social. Only some act crazy. Make it hard for the decent ones."

Steven put aside his tentative report. He had to admit they had nothing concrete. At present, his time should be fully occupied with the Ancell murder. Such a dull murder!

77

He had told Kylie it looked like a domestic murder despite the items stolen from the shop. That meant Luke Ancell, who had so obviously lied when he was being interviewed. Or perhaps Hugo Benson who owed $3,000 to Carter Ancell.

Unless they unearthed someone else with a better reason it looked as though they could concentrate on these two. A little more digging, a little more probing, and in the next day or so they could be making an arrest.

He waited till Peacock was ready to go to Wainui again, commandeered a car and they set off towards the eastern hills.

Another hot day! The cool waters of the harbour were ruffled by an off-shore breeze, sparkling the cobalt with gleams of silver. Soon they were over the top of the hill with the whole Wainui valley spread drowsily before them.

As they drove down towards the patrol base and the Mall, Steven looked across at the site of yesterday's fire.

It stood out like a festering sore amongst the drab grey-green of the sun-scorched gorse—gorse that, in flower, painted the hills with gold. Now it was a fire hazard.

The fireboys had been lucky to contain the blaze so quickly. An outbreak of that intensity and suddenness often took days to bring under control, days in which any maverick wind fanned the flames over a larger and larger acreage. Fortunately the wind had been comparatively light yesterday. Fortunately. Otherwise there would still be men out there, working over the slopes, fighting to keep the menace within bounds.

When they reached the patrol base, they found the last of the reports from details operating around the Mall, around the area where Carter Ancell had lived. All routine. All time consuming. All vitally necessary to any such inquiry.

Steven went through them carefully, summarising, picking out items that needed further clarification, working alone in the patrol base because today only he and Jonas had come over to work with Driscoll. All the leg work had been done, but minor odds and ends still required their presence.

Lower Hutt rang to say the coroner had received the pathologist's report, had set the inquest for two o'clock Friday. Would he notify Luke Ancell and Hugo Benson. The inquest would be brief—establishing identity, cause of death then adjourned.

Steven dropped what he was doing, glad for the opportunity to stretch his legs even if only to go to the Mall.

Shoppers were already about making a colourful tableau. The

promotion court was being prepared for a display of small sailing craft. Ancell's had the door open which meant either Luke or Mrs Martin had decided to carry on the business.

Steven paused to glance in at the window, at the same time looking through into the shop. Mrs Martin was showing some exciting glass sculpture to an enthusiastic-looking customer. Steven entered. Mrs Martin raised her eyebrows, nodded towards the office. Steven smiled his thanks, walked towards the mirror wall.

Luke was sitting on a high stool at the narrow bench below the one-way glass. He gave Steven a brief white smile, said quietly, "Half expected you along some time today, Sergeant."

He indicated a chair for Steven, who preferred to lean against the bench. From there he had a good view of the shop, could also glance casually at the papers in front of Luke without appearing to be snooping.

Apparently Luke was doing a stocktaking, which would be necessary under the circumstances. Now, he pushed the papers aside, leaned his chin on his palms, waited for Steven to speak.

"Came to tell you the inquest's tomorrow at two o'clock. Coroner expects you there. Next of kin. Identifying the body. That sort of thing. The finding will be left open because we're still investigating."

Luke nodded. "Good. Means I can finalise funeral arrangements. Something." He sat there, gazing out at the shop, lost in some secret thoughts of his own.

Steven, watching him, felt dismissed. He had delivered his message. Now he could go. Perversely he refused to take the hint, said amiably, "You missed all the excitement yesterday."

"So I believe. Nothing unusual. Get a couple of burns every year in the summer. Stupid kids trying to show off." His voice was flat, indifferent, not exactly encouraging further conversation.

Steven persisted. "How did it go with you yesterday? Did you straighten out all your suppliers?"

"More or less. Gave them the facts anyway."

"That you'd be taking over?"

Luke gave him a cool blue stare. "I checked with Uncle Car's lawyer first. He told me I inherit. That gave me an edge. I mean, I could talk to the suppliers, let them know everything would be business as usual. That's why I needed to see them. Personal contact's much more effective."

"Why the lawyer? You said you knew you'd be inheriting. Did you have second thoughts?"

"No. Just wanted to be sure. After all, the last time I saw Uncle

79

Car he was pretty mad at me. Could've changed his will." He sighed. "I was going to crawl back next Friday anyway. His birthday, y'know."

"No. I didn't know. Though I suppose we do have it on record. You said the last time you saw your uncle. When exactly?"

Luke flicked a blue glance at Steven, said softly, "Last week. He came round to the flat but I wasn't home. Mrs Tollings next door told me he'd been there—wanted to see me. I went up to his house. Y'know, on Fitzherbert Road."

"Yes. We know. We've also made intensive house-to-house inquiries in that area as you can guess."

Luke smiled thinly. "So you knew we'd had another row? I bet someone around there heard us slanging each other. But that's all it was. You can cut a person to pieces with words." Sombre eyes, bitter voice.

"Luke, when we asked you when you last saw your uncle you said three weeks ago. When you quit and took this job with Wright's. Now you admit seeing him last Thursday. Why? Because you realised we knew about your visit to your uncle's house? What about Monday night? D'you still say you didn't see your uncle Monday night?"

"No. I was half way to New Plymouth when all that happened." No hesitation. No second thoughts. A positive statement. Yet Steven felt he was lying. Knew he was lying. Well, a little more rope—

Steven straightened, took a step towards the door, paused. "What time did you get back last night?" he asked casually.

"Around ten. Half-past. After I'd tidied up my business I went up to my aunt's for tea."

"Your aunt? I thought Carter Ancell was your only relative."

"No, I said I was *his* only kin. Besides Aunt Mary's not a blood relation. A great friend of my mother, that's all. But I do have a couple of uncles. My mother's brothers."

"Yes, of course. Forgot about that aspect. Threw me for a minute. Well, if you think of anything else, let us know."

"I'll do that," said Luke absently, hands reaching for the discarded papers. He did not look up again as Steven left but Steven knew he was being watched through the one-way glass.

His next call was on Benson, who hurried him into the tiny office at the back of the shop, closed the door on him. He had recovered from his surliness of the day before, treated Steven affably, almost seemed pleased to see him. Steven told him about the inquest,

explained procedure, went into unnecessary detail fully aware
Benson was bursting to say something himself.

At last he relented, allowed Benson to speak. The man wanted
to know about the fire. He had heard a rumour that a child had
nearly perished in the blaze. Was it true? Steven told him the story
of Shane's rescue.

When Benson heard the name an odd look came into his eyes.
Judy Lismore, he said, was a friend of his daughter. She had had
a rough time with that brutal husband of hers. He was glad nothing
had happened to Shane. Very glad.

Now he had Benson in a co-operative mood, Steven touched
lightly on the matter that had caused so much friction the day
before. "I suppose you've made arrangements to pay that overdue
loan. Probably have to be done anyway—to wind up the estate."

Benson was tight-lipped with embarrassment, resentful at being
reminded. "No. I thought I'd talk to Luke. Arrange something."

"You knew that Luke would inherit, of course."

"Well, of course. The sun and moon shone out of Luke as far
as Carter was concerned."

"But they'd quarrelled. Bitterly. Seemingly irrecoverably. Luke
had even quit the shop."

Benson pulled a face. "Yeh, I know. But Carter was a fair
man. And blood is always thicker than water, Sergeant."

Steven nodded. "What was Carter Ancell's attitude to his nephew,
Mr Benson? You must've been in a good position to judge."

Benson looked puzzled. "I don't know what you mean exactly.
He thought of Luke as the son he never had, y'know."

"Well, in that case, fatherly would be the word, wouldn't it? But
how fatherly? Protective? Maybe even over-protective?"

"You can say that again," chortled Benson. "Whenever that red-
haired harpy over the way tried to make a pass at Luke, old Carter
would be after her like a bull terrier protecting his pup."

"Most young men would find that embarrassing."

Benson laughed. "Didn't seem to worry Luke any. Maybe he
preferred it. A bit woman-shy, I think. Scared stiff of Sheila when
she was steaming. A lot of woman. Frighten even an old codger like
me if she laid it on the line the way she did with Luke." He sounded
a trifle regretful that Sheila had not laid it on the line with him.

Steven chuckled inwardly as he crossed the promotion court but
the red-haired harpy was strangely reticent when he questioned her.
She kept saying she thought Luke was a nice boy—that Carter
coddled him too much—that now he had a chance to prove he was

a man. Beyond that she would not go. Her eyes kept darting towards the novelty shop as though watching for Luke, watching, waiting, for a chance to pounce now the protective shield of Carter Ancell had been removed.

Yet somehow she gave Steven the impression that the spice had gone out of the game. She even behaved as she looked, a busy manageress with too much on her mind. Maybe the police attitude of indifference to her opulent charms had had the desired effect.

Back at the base, Steven found a report from Wanganui, realised he had spoken to Luke too soon. The report stated baldly that Luke's car had been seen parked to the south of Virginia Lake as stated—but on Wednesday morning. The car had been noted by a passing patrol but as it was not on any suspect list no action was taken. Sighting definitely Wednesday morning at 2 a.m. There was no reported sighting on Tuesday morning although the area was a normal checking point by night patrols.

They had not actually asked Luke when he had left New Plymouth, but he had inferred that he had come straight home after ringing Driscoll. The motel said he checked out at 10.05 p.m. Tuesday after some telephone calls. If he had come straight home he should have arrived about 3 a.m. Wednesday. Mrs Tollings said 6.30 a.m. Now Transport said he was sleeping in his car at Virginia Lake at 2 a.m.

Steven thought about Luke as he had looked in the office of Ancell's Gifts and Novelties. Wearing blue today, soft blue overshirt, deeper blue shorts, that silver Gemini medallion around his throat, on his right wrist a chunky name bracelet in textured gold.

Benson said he was woman-shy. Sheila Bungay called him a nice boy, did not try to hide her fascination. Well, Luke was one out of the box all right—perfect features, heavy-lashed blue eyes, blue-black hair. Appeal to any woman. Any woman?

Steven was still gazing at the report when Peacock came in, gave him a hard look, eased himself on to the corner of the desk, asked gruffly, "Anything interesting?"

Steven brought him up to date finishing with the traffic report. Peacock shrugged. "Sounds like an alibi of sorts. Went wrong. Got his nights mixed up."

Steven nodded doubtfully, hesitated, decided it was now or never. "What words would you use to describe Luke Ancell?" he asked abruptly.

Peacock looked at him shrewdly. "Pretty. Beautiful even. That what you want?"

"More or less. And Carter Ancell? Assertive? Aggressive? Over-protective? Anyway he fought with that tigress across the way every time she tried to lay the boy." Mentally he realised he was reacting to Luke the same way most people did—little boy Luke.

"Jealousy, you reckon? Could be. Classic relationship."

Their speculation was interrupted by the entrance of Driscoll with a quiet request. "Mrs Lismore would like to speak to you, sir."

Peacock slipped off the edge of the desk, surprised, moved around to the chair. "Show her in, Driscoll."

Judy Lismore entered, blonde, hazel-eyed, bare arms and long legs tanned to exactly the right shade of bronze to glow against the sun colour of her dress. She came into the room like a burst of sunlight, smiled prettily as Peacock leaped forward, guided her to a vacant chair.

"How's the little boy, Mrs Lismore? Fully recovered, I hope."

"Yes. They kept him in hospital overnight—just in case. I—I stayed there with him. They allow that in certain cases. But he's—well, he's just as though nothing ever happened. Except for the bruise on his forehead."

Peacock beamed. "The young recover quickly, thank goodness."

"Yes—but that's not what I came to see you about. I mean—I'm very grateful for what your men did for me—and Shane—yesterday—and I thought, well, I thought it was only fair I should be straight with you."

The two men regarded her solemnly, waited. She matched their steady gaze, drew a deep breath, said with a rush, "I came about Mr Ancell's death. I know what you're thinking about Luke. I mean, being the one to gain and everything. But Luke couldn't have done it. He was with me that night."

"With you!" Steven had never seen Peacock so shaken.

"Yes. Y'see, I'm separated. The divorce is going through right now. When it's final, well, Luke and I plan to marry."

Peacock recovered swiftly. "Luke said he went to New Plymouth that night."

"Well, yes, he did. Go to New Plymouth, I mean. But he came to my place first. He—he came about ten o'clock. Left about three. He said the trip would take him around five hours. That's why he left at three."

"But why didn't Luke tell us that?"

"He didn't want me involved. I mean, in case John—John Lismore—heard about it. He might've used it to get custody of Shane. At least that's what we were afraid of."

She sat there looking as guilty as hell. A nice girl, thought Steven, caught up in something beyond her control. He wondered why a pretty-boy like Luke had been attracted to a girl like this. Older than him obviously. Not beautiful. Mouth too large—chin too small—but her hazel eyes were direct and candid and there was an air of restfulness about her, a calmness—maturity perhaps—something that the too-young Luke needed.

"That is always a possibility," said Peacock gravely. "Does Luke know you've come to see us?"

"No." She bit her lip, played with the half-dozen silver-wire bracelets she wore on her left wrist. "I just thought it was time you knew. Luke rang me Tuesday night. He told me—no matter what happened—I wasn't to—to get in touch with him or anything. We'd keep away from each other until—until this was all cleared up."

She made a little pleading gesture with her hands.

"I mean, well, we've kept it secret right until now. It wouldn't matter keeping quiet a little longer. Only I thought—well, when I lost Shane I went straight to Mr Driscoll. I mean, we always turn to the police when we need help, don't we? Yet when you need our help, all too often we just don't want to be involved. Anyway, if you arrested Luke, I would've had to come forward. I couldn't let that happen when I knew—when I knew it was all wrong."

Peacock's eyes were hooded, revealing nothing. "You were the girl who rang Driscoll and told him Luke was out of town?" She nodded, remained silent. "And I presume the big row Luke had with his uncle was over you?"

"Yes. I'm afraid so. Luke thought it time to tell Uncle Carter. He was quite surprised by his uncle's reaction. I mean—he told Luke to keep away from me. I was a sinful woman—a loose woman. He called me Jezebel, I think the name was. But he's—he was so old-fashioned. He just didn't understand. I mean, as far as he was concerned, I was married, so Luke should keep away. He thought the world of Luke, y'know. And I suppose, well, the fact that Luke was in love with me was a kind of imperfection. That's why Luke thought it best to get away from him for a while. He thought it would all blow over with time."

"Did you think so?"

She avoided his eyes. "Well, I hoped so, yes. They were too close to hold grudges too long."

In a firmer voice, she said, "But at the same time I told Luke maybe we *were* rushing things. It might be better to put it off for a little longer. The marriage, I mean. Even a year or more. So Uncle

Carter could get to know me better. To know I wasn't—I wasn't the kind of woman he thought I was. Y'see, it was important to me, too. I wanted Uncle Carter to like me. For his sake. For Luke's sake. In no way was I going to come between them. They were very close, y'know. Very close."

Peacock nodded. "Yes. I believe he looked on Luke as his son. A man wants the best for his son but most of all he wants him to be happy. So perhaps you were right. Perhaps he would've come to accept you." He paused. "And if he didn't?"

She twisted her hands unhappily. "I don't know. I hadn't thought that far ahead. But if it came to the point, I guess I could've worked something out so—so they would be reconciled."

Peacock did not pursue the subject. Instead he became extremely matter of fact, brought the conversation back to its original subject. "Now—at exactly what time did Luke arrive at your place on Monday night?"

"At ten past ten. Actually he was late. He was going to be there by half past nine and I thought—I thought, maybe he wasn't coming. But he did come. At ten past ten."

"You didn't ring to see if he was coming?"

"Oh, no. Luke wouldn't like that. Besides, if he'd decided against coming, he would've rung me."

Perhaps, thought Steven. They checked times with Judy Lismore once again, then let her go, thanking her for coming forward.

Jonas leaned back. "Well, what d'you think?"

"I'm thinking Luke could've told us all that. Saved us a bit of time and bother."

Jonas smiled. "Luke's a bit brighter than you think. Don't you see? He didn't want that girl to talk because it gives him another motive for getting rid of Carter."

"Maybe. But if he was at Judy Lismore's place at ten past ten—"

"Oh, come *on*. Carter died around eleven. Yes. But Doc says not immediately. An hour, an hour and a half to die. We know where Carter was at nine-thirty—maybe even nine-forty—talking to Andrew Bartlett. My guess is he was attacked just before ten. Or just after. Mrs Tollings says Luke left the flats that night at about twenty to ten. Didn't arrive at Judy Lismore's place till ten past. Another thing. We still don't know why Carter went back to the shop that night. To meet Luke? To meet Benson? Until we get an answer to that one, we don't know anything."

CHAPTER IX

DRISCOLL CAME IN with more paper work, mostly about pets kept by people living close to Carter Ancell. Several cats but only two dogs, an Alsatian and a Dachshund. There were three envelopes attached. One contained hairs from Carter Ancell's cat, the others hairs from the dogs. A waste of time because Forensic was looking for a long-haired species.

Steven rang the laboratory. They were now able to tell him the dog hairs probably came from a Sydney Silky or something similar. A Sydney Silky? Not exactly a popular breed right now. How many would there be in the valley? If any? Maybe the Ranger could tell him. The council office was in the Mall. Might be a good idea to call in, make a few inquiries.

The telephone rang. Jonas answered, crisp-voiced, sure. He replaced the receiver, swore roundly. "The Anderson case!" he snarled. "Come unstuck. I'll take the car. You can hitch a ride back with the patrol car when it comes through."

He went on to outline the various jobs he wanted Steven to finalise. He himself was going to see what he could do to salvage the Anderson case.

The Anderson case—involving a scrap merchant named Anderson and a storeman at a local factory. Police had been watching Anderson, knowing he was receiving stolen property, unable to prove it. When they discovered this storeman pocketing proceeds of scrap sales made to Anderson they had used this as a basis for a receiving charge.

On trial now, Anderson was claiming he was an innocent caught up in a change of office procedure. Previously he had paid on invoices based on weighbridge certificates. Six months ago the storeman told him the new instruction was that he had to pay before he could take the scrap steel. This was routine in his line of business so he had not suspected anything out of order, had immediately started paying on the weighbridge certificates as he did with most of his other clients. Until told by police he had not known the storeman was not passing his payments on to front office.

Plausible and straightforward. A matter of his word against that of the storeman who had already been convicted for stealing as a servant. What Jonas hoped to do, Steven could not guess. He did not rate his chances too highly. By the time Jonas arrived back in Lower Hutt, the trial would probably be well over, Anderson acquitted "without a stain on his character". Well, you win some, you lose some, so what!

Steven returned to the Ancell case. He went to the council office but the clerk could not help him. Dog licences were issued but not analysed. Only by a search of records could such a fact be established. It would take a great deal of work. Was it really necessary? Steven reluctantly admitted probably not.

He called in at Ancell's to find Mrs Martin in charge. Luke had taken the early lunch break, would be back at twelve-thirty. They took turns so there was always someone at the shop.

Steven went on to talk to Townsend about the burglar alarm. Wiseman wanted more details, timing, structure, everything. He obtained the information, was about to go back to the base when he felt a crinkling in his pocket, remembered the letter Kylie had given him to post that morning.

Instead of turning right, he turned left towards the post office. As he passed the cafeteria and take-away bar he saw a familiar head of black hair, looked at his watch. Quarter to twelve. A bit early but why not?

Without another thought he entered the cafeteria, picked up a tray, selected his lunch, paid for it, walked over to where Luke was sitting at a two-person formica-topped table close to the far wall. He indicated the vacant chair.

"D'you mind if I sit here?" he asked.

Luke shrugged. "Help yourself. Not my property."

Steven sat down, made a performance of setting out the plate with two sandwiches and one hot meat pattie, the bottle of grapefruit juice, finally placed the tray on the floor behind his chair.

Luke's table was almost private, surrounded by others as yet unoccupied. Most of the customers filled the other end of the long oblong room, mothers with small children, middle-aged women in groups. Steven hoped their comparative seclusion would last long enough for him to finish his talk with Luke although he guessed he would not have too much time.

Already a line was forming at the serve-yourself counter but probably most would be for takeaway foods.

"D'you eat here often?" Steven asked cheerfully.

Luke looked at him obliquely. "Not too often. A snack now and then. But the food's okay. If that's all you want."

Steven smiled, bit into the meat pattie. It was absolutely right, pastry light and flaky, filling meaty and full of flavour. He sipped thoughtfully at the fruit juice, watched Luke pulling a sandwich to shreds. After a moment Luke realised he was under scrutiny, made an effort to push some of the shredded bread into his mouth. Evidently he had no appetite, was simply going through the motions.

"We had a visit from Judy Lismore this morning," Steven said chattily.

Luke stiffened, relaxed. "I told her to keep out of it."

"So we believe. But it would've saved us a lot of trouble if you'd been truthful in the beginning." Luke was silent. "We also had a report from Transport. They did notice your car at Virginia Lake. Wednesday morning at 2 a.m. Not Tuesday morning as you led us to believe." Luke shrugged. "What did you hope to gain by that, Luke? Trying to build yourself an alibi?"

"Sort of. Thought maybe just to be seen there would do it. They mightn't remember which night."

"They remembered. You picked that place because you knew patrols keep it under observation. Been there before, eh?"

No answer.

"Unfortunately for you, Luke, whenever an officer notices something he puts it on his day sheet. And they're numbered, dated, handed in each day. So it didn't help you any."

"I didn't want Judy involved," he mumbled. "It wasn't fair."

"She told us that. But we can be very discreet when we want to be, Luke. If you'd been honest with us in the beginning we probably wouldn't have gone beyond asking Judy to confirm." He took another sip of the juice. "All right. Now we've got that straightened out, suppose you start with Monday night again."

Luke looked at him inquiringly.

"Well, did you or did you not see your uncle on Monday night? The truth this time."

Luke shook his head. "I didn't see him. I tried to see him. Wanted to be able to tell Judy he was softening. Some hope! But that was the idea. No, I didn't see him. He wasn't at home."

"You went into the house?"

"No. Didn't need to. No lights. Sox roaming around outside. If Uncle Car had been home the light would've been on in his study. Sox would've been inside. With him."

"He could've gone to bed."

"Too early. He always read till midnight. In his study. I was there, oh, about quarter to ten. Sat in the car waiting but he didn't come. And I knew Judy would be wondering so, come five past, I gave it away."

"You talk about his cat, Sox. Mrs Fulton next door says he was very fond of the cat. I can understand that. A form of companionship. But why not a dog?"

"A dog? No. Have to tie it up during the day while he was at the shop. Uncle Car would consider that an act of cruelty."

"Tell me about your uncle, Luke. We've been able to get only bits and pieces so far. He never married, did he?"

"No."

"Never wanted to marry?"

"Wouldn't know about that."

"Luke—was your uncle gay?"

Luke's face whitened. Tiny lines etched their bitterness around his mouth. His eyes blazed angrily. In a voice low and hate-filled, he spat at Steven, "You filthy police bastard! Can't you leave a decent man alone!"

Steven waited quietly, munching on the ham sandwich. The sweaty look passed from Luke's face. His lips quivered. He looked as though he wanted to be sick.

Steven said gently, "Just the way things look and no one's talking. Sometimes you can do a dead man more harm by keeping quiet than by offering explanations. So—suppose you tell me about Uncle Carter. So far we've established he wasn't gay."

"Even that might've been better. Something positive anyway." Luke swallowed, looked defiantly at Steven. "Uncle Car wasn't anything. He was—he was neuter, I suppose you'd call it."

He was quiet for a moment. "He went to the war, y'know. Shot up like nobody's business and lost—well, when he came back he wasn't a man. That way. Every other way he was a man. Straight as a die. Strong. Courageous. Kind. That's why he didn't marry, mister. He believed in marriage. And family. He believed in all that. But he knew it was not for him. That's why he took an interest in me, I suppose. Next best thing."

Luke toyed with his bits of broken bread. "When I was a kid, I used to wish he was my dad because—well, you know about my dad, don't you, Sergeant? The village stud. Used to lay every sleazy bitch around. Thought it made him a helluva fellow. And I guess the type of company he kept it meant something. But that sort of thing doesn't sit too well inside the family unit, I can tell you. Mum used to cry a lot. And the kids at school! They all knew about it." He spoke with a controlled ferocity, voice pitched so low that Steven could barely hear him, knew no one else could possibly overhear.

"And your Uncle Carter?"

"Uncle Car—well, he'd try talking to dad about it. Be laughed at for his pains. Dad used to ask him what he knew about being a man. That sort of thing. And Uncle Car. Well, it sort of crushed him. Even when I was too young to understand what dad meant, I knew it was something dreadful from the way Uncle Car looked when dad trotted this out.

"When I was old enough to understand—well, I wanted so much to make up for all the rottenness dad dished out to him. Oh, I know Uncle Car was a bit prissy. Old-fashioned. Strait-laced. All of that. But if I'd had a chance to pick the man I wanted for a father, I know the one I'd choose."

He grimaced, voice lifting. "Y'know, I didn't feel anything when dad was killed. Except relief in a way. It meant I wouldn't have to put up with his snide remarks. Oh, yes, I got those all right. Y'see, I sort of shied clear of girls. Mostly because of the way dad carried on. He couldn't understand that. His son. Thought I'd be in for my chops as soon as I was old enough but—" He paused. "Maybe I was scared people would tag me chip off the old block. Y'see, I'd heard some of the dirtier remarks he had missed and, frankly, I didn't want to be like him. No way. So no matter how much he prodded me, I wouldn't play it his way. When he was killed, it was like—a release almost. I'd lived under the cloud of his reputation all my life. Now I was free of it. Yet, when Uncle Car died—it was different. All this emptiness. This lostness. More especially because we weren't exactly friends when it happened."

He stopped abruptly, looked at Steven with those blue, blue eyes. "I didn't kill Uncle Car, Sergeant. I don't know who did or why. But please believe me! It's the last thing I'd do."

Steven nodded. On the face of it, things did look that way but stubbornly in the back of his mind he kept remembering that old refrain—you always hurt the one you love.

Could be Luke had loved the old man too well. And what exactly had Carter Ancell said when he had discovered his nephew's liaison

90

with Judy Lismore? Had he told Luke he was turning into a womaniser like his father? To Luke that would be the unforgivable insult, the one thing he could not tolerate, the thing that would bring a reflex action—a hand groping for a weapon, finding it, hitting, hitting—

Steven could almost visualise the scene. Luke, livid with shocked anger, the old man pious, over-righteous, because he wanted to save Luke from the taint of his father's blood. Perhaps Luke never meant to kill his uncle but— There were too many buts.

"Was there much pain?" Steven asked softly.

"Some. He didn't talk about it but some days there he'd come into the shop looking like death. I'd know then he'd had a bad night. And—" he added ruefully, "I'd know I would be in for a bad day because he'd be pretty short-tempered, easily riled. Still, I knew why so mostly I'd just let it wash over me. Some days, of course, I wouldn't be feeling up to scratch myself. I'd snap back. Then we'd have a real set-to. To an outsider—" he shrugged.

Steven finished his snack, left Luke still crumbling bread on his plate, went along to the post office to post Kylie's letter, returned to the base. His first action was to ring Lower Hutt, ask for David Galt.

"Hi, David. Has the full pathology report arrived yet?"

"Yeh. A while back. Murder. No doubt about it."

"What about the first bit? Condition of the body and so on?"

"Oh, yes, that. Poor devil!" He read the beginning of the report, about Carter Ancell's wound, decked out in medical terms, including an estimate of pain suffered daily.

Steven replaced the receiver. It was a pity Bob Whittaker had had to go to that science congress. His assistant was as qualified, could do the work as well, render an equally full and explicit report but he was not a close friend of Peacock. Bob would have rung Jonas with that piece of news immediately whereas his assistant had considered including the information in the final report was sufficient.

Funny no one in the Mall had mentioned it. But why should they? They believed police would learn about it from the autopsy. Those who knew about it. Benson, possibly. Mrs Martin? Carter kept himself to himself, according to Benson. Constant niggling pain would drain any man's resources but Carter did not discuss personal matters, failings, with anyone, showed a serene face to the world except when disagreeing on matters of policy—as at the

91

monthly meetings. Some days he came in looking like death, Luke said. Those days the outward mask must have slipped. Even then his colleagues could see he was ill, would not necessarily associate that with a war wound, something that had happened over thirty years ago.

Steven wondered what else was being hidden. He remembered the odd look that had come into Benson's eyes when he learned the identity of the missing child.

Judy was a friend of his daughter, he had said. It was reasonable to assume he knew of Luke's attachment. Yet when he spoke of Luke's quarrels with his uncle Benson had allowed the police to believe it was all over business matters.

Steven felt a twinge of annoyance at this sidestepping by both Mrs Martin and Benson. Too often police found good intentions the greatest stumbling block in their search for the truth.

Steven spent the rest of the afternoon trying to confirm Luke's statement that he had waited outside Carter's house for twenty minutes.

The Fultons could not help. Their favourite TV programme was on between 9.30 and 10.30 p.m. Steven went knocking on doors to hear much the same story. Either residents were watching TV or had already gone to bed. No one had seen or heard Luke's car.

There was nothing to prove that Luke had not met his uncle at the Mall, gone with him into the shop, quarrelled again. On the other hand, there seemed to be no valid reason why Luke should meet his uncle at the Mall instead of at his house—unless it was something that required his presence in the shop.

The patrol car came through the valley at five, picked up Steven, took him back to Lower Hutt. Steven reported to a half-listening Jonas, went along to talk burglar alarms with Rex Wiseman.

Once again they went over all the information they had on the elusive Cheapskate.

Carefully they compared his break-ins with the happening at the Mall, noting the similarities, the differences. By the time they finished Steven felt he had been reading the same script over and over. He went home in a disgruntled mood that Kylie found unnecessary and she did not hesitate to say so.

"For heaven's sake, why d'you let it churn you up so much? Once you've left work, forget about it. Relax. You're home now. Get yourself around that steak and stop talking shop."

Even as she said it, she probably realised he could not put everything out of his mind so easily. Obediently, he sat down, enjoying the meal in an absent-minded way, steak with mushrooms followed by lemon meringue.

Afterwards, he found himself dawdling, pushing a fork around on the tablecloth as Kylie was clearing the table. She sat down opposite him, forced him to look at her.

"It's Luke, isn't it? You don't want it to be Luke. But think about it. You always tell your men not to let themselves get involved. Isn't that just what you're doing?"

"Perhaps. It's not just that. The case is so shapeless. Little bits and pieces that don't mean a thing yet they spoil the whole picture. Throw it all out of kilter."

"But you think Luke—"

"Well, we could build a good case against Luke. Yes. We'd have to say the jewellery was taken to confuse the issue. To give the impression Carter Ancell had surprised a burglar."

He laughed derisively. "And Luke's defence would be that Carter Ancell *did* surprise a burglar. A burglar known to the police as Cheapskate. The court would throw our case out."

The trouble with murder was it was usually one-off. Any other crime was repetitive. Thieves were seldom caught on their first sally into crime. More often they managed to escape with the spoils, thinking they had done something clever to outwit police. What they did not seem to understand was that with every burglary they committed, the more chance of capture.

Files would be compiled around each operation, similarities checked, conclusions drawn, until suddenly the finger pointed. The culprit would then be brought in for questioning or, maybe, simply watched, to be caught redhanded—and given the option of owning up to all the crimes listed against his name. That way often old outstanding thefts could be wiped off the record as solved with one capture.

Cheapskate was different. Careful. Never greedy. Took only stuff he knew could not be definitely sworn to as being the property of any particular shop. He was also clever in that he seemed to know all about any premises he entered, knew and bypassed burglar alarm systems, was not above using various professional means of entry to confuse the investigators. He probably also knew they would have to catch him in the act otherwise the chances of proving he was Cheapskate were practically nil.

Now he was suspected of murder.

Would he accept that—knowing they could not touch him—

believing they could not touch him. Steven wondered idly how close he might be to the Wainui Mall people. Could be one of them even. Maybe that was why Carter Ancell died. Because he recognised Cheapskate. Or perhaps because he quarrelled once too often with Luke. Or Hugo Benson. Or—

Steven sighed, realising the course his mind was travelling, looked at Kylie. "All right. I'll be a good boy. Tai'll be here shortly. Give me something else to think about."

Kylie frowned. "Yes, I know. But it's still shop. So why don't you read or something? Do something entirely different. Make yourself think about something else." She took the cloth off the table, looked at the clock. "Maureen's expecting me tonight. But I won't be long. Be back before Tai leaves. Okay?"

Steven nodded, wandered into the front room, stretched himself on the lounge, picked up the paper. He did the crossword puzzle to empty his mind completely, read the overseas news, the editorial, dutifully skipped all reports headed by anything that looked like police material, was reading the sports pages when Kylie called goodbye and left the house.

What now? His attention focused on a short article headed "Protection for Rare Samba Deer". He could not believe it. Protection for deer—in New Zealand where the deer was classed as a noxious animal.

Carefully he read through the article.

It seemed the manager of a Land and Survey Department property near Foxton, a small town about eighty miles north on the west coast, had joined forces with the local Deerstalkers Association to save the small herd of samba deer that roamed the 5,000 acres. They wanted the deer classified as protected until the numbers built up to a secure limit.

Steven pushed the paper away from him. Last week there had been a report from the Forest Research people stating that 90 per cent of deer had been cleared from certain national forest areas by the use of helicopter hunting. Not samba deer, of course, but still— In the North Island they were trying to protect deer while in the South Island they were trying to exterminate them.

Steven thought about hunting from helicopters. Hardly sporting but the hunters were not doing it for sport. They had built up a good export trade in venison, shipping out in a peak year over 10,000 carcases. Helicopters carrying slain deer were a familiar sight to people living near the Fiordland National Park. So much so that deer farms were the latest thing, controlled farming of an imported pest. Now helicopter hunters shot deer with tranquilliser darts, bringing them back alive.

His thoughts were interrupted by a knock. He bounded to his feet, opened the door expecting to see the broad face of Tai Bennett. It was not Tai. It was Rob Henshawe, standing there with a friendly smile in his grey eyes.

CHAPTER X

FOR A SECOND Steven stared at Rob in surprise, then he remembered his manners. "Why, come on in, Rob. I don't see you for ages then it's twice in a couple of days."

"I hope you don't mind," said Rob stepping inside, eyes searching the unfamiliar room. "Is Kylie in?"

"No. She's off down the street to see a friend. Won't be long though. Did you want to see her? I can ring."

"No. No. It's you I want to see. But if Kylie had been here . . ." He shrugged, looked at Steven squarely. "First, I'd like to apologise for barging in like that at Delacourt's. I had no business doing that but, well, it seemed the right thing at the time."

"And so it was!" said Steven heartily, ushering him into the front room. "Take a pew and let's have a yarn about old times."

He regretted the words as soon as they were spoken. Fortunately, Rob did not seem to notice. He shook his head.

"That's not what I'm here for. It's just—" He swung away from Steven, walked over to the picture window, stood with his back to the room gazing out at the silver birch trees moving languidly in the evening breeze. "I didn't need to do that, Steven. I knew about the two signature thing beforehand. Had Frank Summerfield lined up for one, my uncle for the other. He runs the factory over the road from Delacourt's. But when I saw you—it was like a sign. Like it was meant."

He turned back into the room, walked over to the chair, sat down opposite Steven.

"Look, Steven. Before it—before I left the force I was working with the break squad. Not officially—but Rex was short-handed and he roped me in. I liked it. Something different. Interesting. Anyway, there's a character the squad called Cheapskate. Heard of him? D'you know if he's been picked up yet?"

"I've heard of him. He hasn't been nailed yet."

"No. He's a wily one. Plays it real cool. Well, he specialises in medium-priced fashion jewellery. Hits mostly smaller shops. This job I did with Rex—first time he'd hit the Hutt. Svensen's—at the other end of High Street. Rex had me analysing the things he'd taken. And I guess, because it was my first dig at anything like that, I was noticing details." He licked his lips. "Steven, I've got an idea about Cheapskate."

He stopped suddenly, eyes searching Steven's face for the least flicker of amusement.

Steven said solemnly, "So you've got an idea. Tell me."

"I think he could be a company rep. Great cover. No, wait a minute. You met Frank Summerfield—the guy with me? Well, he's the one made me think like that. When I took on this job, I worked with Frank for a week to get the hang of it. Everywhere we went, he'd bring out this little packet of fashion jewellery, sell to any female around, on farms, in country towns, hotels, stores. Real bargain stuff. He's got quite a reputation for bargain stuff."

"You think Frank Summerfield—?"

"No. No. Wait a moment. Not Frank. But he did put the idea into my head. Some of the prices he charged seemed way down. I asked him how he managed it and he said it was a come-on really. Sometimes he would let a piece go at cost just to get customer confidence. But he'd sure as hell make up for it on the next piece—or the next. It paid off in the long run because everywhere there'd be people he'd given something really cheap. And, as he says, people are funny about fashion jewellery. They'll pay up to $30 without turning a hair if the piece looks worth it but once past $30 they tighten their purse-strings. Of course, he always has this chatter about the things being well below shop prices—which they are. Another trick he showed me was bringing out a recent invoice to show the customer they're legit."

"I see. Now you've gone in for this, too?"

"Too right. First of all, Frank carried me. Got me stuff through his own account at Delacourt's. Told me what prices to charge. Some of the chatter. Just to see how it went. No actual commitment, y'see. Then I got a few parcels myself for cash. Did all right with those, too. Now I've been accepted as a regular customer with them. Just as well. Paying cash is tough."

"Aha! That explains all that rigmarole yesterday."

Rob smiled. "You're so right. Frank said to stick to Delacourt's because they're also agents for some of the smaller manufacturers. Means they've got quite a range. He also mentioned they already have a few reps on their books. Used to them."

He pulled a face. "That's when it hit me. What's to stop a guy buying jewellery from Delacourt's, nicking the same stuff from a shop or whatever, selling it all under the one legitimate invoice, so to speak."

"Could be. Happens. That case with antique silver. Remember?" Steven lifted an eyebrow. "Not Frank Summerfield though?"

Rob laughed. "No. Not Frank. I thought so in the beginning, mind you. When I saw him flogging that underpriced stuff. But I use that technique myself now. And it works. No, he's not the one. Always been quite open about it. Never carries more than a small parcel."

"He knows you are an ex-cop?"

"Yeh. Known Frank a couple of years now. So he knew me when—when it was all happening." He hesitated. "What d'you think, Steven?"

"It's an interesting theory, Rob. Could be you're right. But how to prove it. Look—Tai Bennett's coming round later. He's with break squad. He'd know about Cheapskate. Maybe you two should get together. Talk it over."

"No." Rob shook his head. "Guess I was just kidding myself. Still thinking like a policeman, eh? It's just, well, it seemed so logical. If you could check some of Delacourt's invoices—"

"Oh, come off it, Rob. On what grounds? A hunch? Delacourt would scream his head off. Police interference and all that."

"I didn't mean holus bolus, Steven. I meant, if we—if I could name a name. Maybe then, eh?"

"Sure. Show us just cause and we'll be in. Boots and all."

After Steven had shown Rob out, he sat back in his chair thinking. It was an interesting theory all right. Plausible. Logical. Delacourt spoke as though there were several travellers selling fashion jewellery as a sideline. One of them could be Cheapskate selling stolen pieces under the curtain of legitimate purchase. Could be.

He found himself thinking about Frank Summerfield. Dark laughing eyes, easy manner, shrewd, con man written all over him. Exactly the type. His speculation was interrupted by the arrival of Tai Bennett.

Tai came in, wiping his face, complaining about the weather. "Hot, isn't she? Worse than last year, I reckon."

Steven laughed. "You told me before Christmas it was going to be another long hot summer."

"Well, sure. Never seen such bloom on cabbage trees in my life.

Remember that one I showed you in Woburn Road. Close on forty feet high, lily sprays way down to five feet. If that's not a sign of a long hot summer, I don't know what is."

He unbuttoned his overshirt, followed Steven into the living-room. Steven left him there, made a quick trip into the kitchen, opened the refrigerator, helped himself to two cans of lager, returned to Tai. "Here's something to help you cool down a bit," he said.

Tai took one of the dewy cans, clipped it, took a long pull. "Ah, that's more like it. Now, I'm ready to talk business." He placed his notebook on the small magazine table with an air of complete satisfaction.

Steven lifted his hand. "Before we start I've got something for the break squad." Briefly he outlined Rob's theory.

Tai grimaced. "Sure, it could be. We've thought of that. Asked manufacturers for lists of customers but, hell, we'd need an army to check up on every shoppie, casual trader, the lot. A better lead was an employee. On five occasions places were hit immediately after receiving a large order from Delacourt's. Suggests inside contact, doesn't it? But when we tried to get Delacourt to co-operate— boy, did he get hot under the collar. I mean, we didn't have a single fact to support our premise. So he wasn't going to have his people pushed around by a bunch of flatfeet for nothing. His very words." Tai laughed softly at the recollection. "Of course, if the powers that be decide Cheapskate did kill Ancell, maybe we'll have to do a bit of arm-twisting. Get him to see reason. Meantime, let's talk about Cody Pyke, eh?"

"Anything much?"

"Nothing helpful. The Star Five club seems legitimate. Old man Pyke opened up as soon as I spoke to him about it. Showed me photographs, letters—or rather post cards. Seems the Star Five is just a social club. The five of them got together to explore. Every time Cody and his cobbers found a new town, he'd drop a post card to the folks, tell them all about it."

"All about it?"

"Yeh, I thought about that. I mean—the bikes, the outfits, patches like the big gangs. Maybe—" He was quiet a moment.

"Just see it, can't you. The five of them descending on a sleepy country town. Strutting around. Taking over the pub. Churning everyone up just by being there. Maybe that's the way they got their kicks. If so, they didn't tell daddy about it."

"Naturally. You said photographs."

"Yeh. With their bikes. Without their bikes. Together. Singly.

Helmets on. Helmets off. All looked reasonably tidy. On the face
of it just a social club. Asa Pyke really believes that. Quite open
about it. Told me where to find Dalziel, the lot. Of course he made
damn sure I understood it was just a get-together club. His son
wouldn't belong to any bikie gang. Not my boy Cody. I asked him
for names but the only one he knew was Dalziel."

"And Dalziel?"

"That was slightly different. I went up to Silverstream where he
lives, told him who I was. Reacted straight away. Said he didn't
talk to fuzz. I explained I was making an unofficial inquiry on
behalf of Cody's parents so he relaxed. Co-operated sort of."

"Sort of?"

"Way he talked. Dead pan. Kind of flat. Like he was watching
every word. Like he didn't want me to be too curious. Sounded as
though he was telling me a lot but when I analysed it afterwards—
just a mass of words. A great talker. Has the gift of the gab all
right. Saying scads without telling you anything."

He chuckled. "Put it across me, he did. But he stuck to the social
club bit for Star Five. I asked for names. He didn't want to give
them at first but his uncle made him. The reason the Star Five broke
up was because the head boy died. Pneumonia. Fellow named
Adam Curry. After that they kind of drifted back to their home
towns. Lost touch with each other."

"You said his uncle was there. Why?"

Tai grinned. "Dalziel's folks died when he was a kid. Uncle and
aunt took him in, brought him up. No kids of their own. Uncle sat
in because I was police. Seems Guy had a brush with the law about
four years ago. Minor league. Bravado stuff then lying to cover.
Uncle thought he'd straightened him out good and proper. That's
why he let him go to Auckland when the firm shifted up there.
Couple of years ago. But it didn't work out. Guy stayed with the
firm only a year then started job-hopping. Finally ended without a
decent job, came back home."

"Auckland? Cody was at Kuwarau."

"Nope. He was at Auckland, too. Never got around to telling
his folks. Yeh, I know his father let us think he was at Kuwarau.
Can't blame him. That's where he thought Cody was. Told everybody that. By the time he found out different, a bit late to change
his tune. Y'see, Cody did go to Kuwarau originally. To work with
Tasman Pulp and Paper Mill. Wrote home often enough. Always
forgot to show an address. Forgot to mention he'd gone on to
Auckland. Accidentally or on purpose. Who knows?"

"Didn't it worry them?"

"No. As long as they heard from him regularly, that was all that mattered. Not exactly a writing family actually. Mother wrote once care of Tasman. Letter returned, address unknown. They thought a lazy clerk not bothering to make inquiries. The mill's a big place."

"Postmarks on the letters?"

"Posted all over. Only one or two letters. Mostly post cards. Sent from towns they visited week-ends. A couple were marked as coming from Auckland. Mostly elsewhere."

Steven felt deflated. They had wasted so much time on nothing. He took the short list Tai gave him, read through the names of the Star Five. Adam Curry, Heta Mairangi, Kara Jones, Cody Pyke, Guy Dalziel. Tai explained they were listed in order of age, Curry the oldest at twenty-five, Dalziel the youngest, just turned twenty-two. Beside Mairangi's name was written Gisborne; beside Jones, Otaki. They certainly were scattered. Otaki was a small town on the west coast, 46 miles north; Gisborne was on the east coast, 340 miles north.

"What did they do with their bikes?" Steven asked casually.

"Cody sold his when he lost his job. So he'd have money to come home with, father said. Didn't ask Dalziel but probably the same. Hasn't got a bike now anyway. Runs an old blue Holden."

"Yeh, I know." Steven read through the names again. It would be natural enough for the club to break up when Curry died. He was probably the strong one, all that held it together. When Dalziel lost his job—and Cody Pyke—home would seem the best place.

The other two—Kara Jones and Heta Mairangi—did they lose their jobs too? At the same time? Kara Jones. He had heard that name before. Some time. Some place.

"Wait a minute. I know that name Kara Jones. Or something damn well like it. Charlie Fenton would know."

He went over to the telephone, dialled Wellington Central Police Station, asked for Sergeant Fenton. He spoke a few minutes. Grimaced, hung up, returned to Tai.

"Charlie wasn't there. They're going to tell him I called. But they told me what I wanted to know. Kara Jones is the name of the guy who broke out of the Williams Building last year. Remember?"

"Really. D'you think it could be the same Kara Jones?"

"Could be. If it is, we're into a new ball game, eh?"

The incident had caused a sensation when it happened. It began casually enough. The night watchman, making his rounds, heard noises coming from an office on the sixth floor. Looking in, he had seen Jones in front of the safe. Quickly he locked the office door, sounded the alarm. When the police contingent arrived they found the would-be burglar's smashed and broken body on the asphalt below the building. In attempting to escape, he had fallen six stories to his death.

There had been inquiries. At one stage, the night watchman was tentatively charged with manslaughter but it was soon proved the man was incapable of overcoming a husky young tough like Jones.

"What d'you reckon?" asked Tai. "Didn't know where he was."

Steven nodded. "That's the general opinion. Means someone else mapped out the job for him, got him into the building, forgot to mention the office was on the sixth floor."

"Accidentally or on purpose."

"Definitely on purpose. If what I'm beginning to believe is true."

Such a thing could only happen in Wellington. The topography of the land with its eternal hills meant a street could run next and parallel to another yet be many feet below.

This was the situation where the Williams Building was located. Erected at the back of a block of land between two streets named Lambton Quay and the Terrace, the first six floors were built against the bank supporting the upper street. Anyone walking into the building from the Terrace entered the sixth floor, would believe it to be the ground floor unless told otherwise. The actual ground floor faced on to Lambton Quay, six floors of glass and concrete below.

When he was trapped by the locking of the door, Kara Jones smashed a window, leaped out, not knowing he was on the Lambton Quay side, that he had nearly eighty feet to fall.

"All right," said Tai slowly. "Let's assume this is the same Kara Jones. That means three of the Five are dead already. Leaves two alive unless— Do we know about Heta Mairangi?"

"That's something we'll have to leave till tomorrow. Don't think Jonas will stop us now. Three out of five is too much of a coincidence. What d'you think? Revenge? A vendetta?"·

Tai gave him a long look, shook his head slowly.

"Guy Dalziel said Curry died of pneumonia. Jones jumped to his death unintentionally. Cody pulled the chip pile down on top of himself. Sickness and accidents."

"Accidents can be arranged," said Steven drily. "And we can't ignore three out of five. Two of them while apparently engaged in some felonious pursuit. Accepting Cody was the one in the car park. Which could mean someone set them up. Which someone? Someone they both knew from their Auckland period. A fixer perhaps. A middleman who'd worked with them before in Auckland. So when he told them of easy pickings down here they fell for it."

Tai nodded gravely. "That's one angle. There's another more obvious possibility. Look at the Star Five. A bikie gang no matter how much Pappa Pyke tries to cover up. Imitators. Yeh, I know perhaps that was all they were. But they ape the tougher gangs. The bad boys. Clothes, high-powered bikes, gang patches, the lot. They do it for kicks. Just how far would they go? What else would they copy to pretend they were as vicious as the worst of them?"

Stevens stared at him. "Oh, my God! You don't mean a block?"

"Possible. What did that stupid goon say in that Auckland trial? 'Blocking was ceremonial. There was no way the pigs were going to stop it.' That particular gang trial must've happened while the Star Five were in Auckland."

The block. Multiple rape. Gang rape. Ceremonial, they claimed. More often, simply viciousness.

Both men were silent, weighing the possibilities.

For some time now, Steven had been aware of sounds in the next room, low voices, women's voices, guessed Kylie had returned. When the door opened he was not entirely surprised.

Kylie stood there, smiling at them. "Hi, fellas. Finished your confab? Feel like a cuppa? Come on. Time to relax. I have someone I want you to meet."

Tai hastily buttoned up his shirt, raised his eyebrows at Steven who shrugged, led the way to the dining room.

There were two other girls there—Maureen McNair whom both Tai and Steven knew, mousey, lathe-thin, bright eyes, and another, vividly dark, shining black hair, big brown eyes, soft young mouth. Kylie introduced her as Tanea Wiata, explained she had recently moved to the North Island to take up a nursing post at the Hutt Hospital.

"Oh," said Steven, "that means you don't know many people up here, I suppose." It also explained that matchmaking look in Kylie's eyes as she introduced Tai.

"Not many. But Maureen says she'll look after that."

"That's good," said Steven solemnly as he seated himself at the table. "And you'll meet plenty of people through your work."

He listened to the chatter going on around him as Kylie poured cups of coffee. Tai, the big ox, suddenly seemed all hands and feet. He was gazing at Tanea as though he had never seen anyone so lovely—tongue-tied, completely out of his depth.

Steven looked at Kylie, winked.

"What branch of nursing, Tanea?" he asked. He had to keep the conversation going even if it was only to cover up for Tai.

"Oh, maternity this time. I skipped it before but it will be a change to go into a ward where no one's sick—more or less."

She accepted her cup from Kylie, spooned in two heaped tea-spoons of sugar. Steven suppressed a chuckle, aware of Kylie's widened eyes, Maureen's look of absolute disbelief. Tanea finished stirring, helped herself to a piece of devil food cake, rich and dark with chocolate. She seemed totally unaware of her effect on Tai. Unaware? She turned her long-lashed eyes to Steven, gave him her full attention. "Maureen says you're a policeman," she said blandly.

"That's right."

"I've met quite a few policemen," she said but did not elaborate. She nibbled thoughtfully at her cake, flirted her eyes at Tai. "And you're police, too, aren't you?"

Tai wet his lips. "Yes," he stammered. "I'm police."

Steven looked at Kylie, smiled, waited for Tanea's next words.

"Maureen says you work with Steven here. Does that mean you're a detective?"

Tai swallowed. "Yes. But—but I'm just starting. Steven's been—well, he's a sergeant. I'm just a constable."

Steven rolled his eyes. "Yes, I'm a real old man," he said. "And we don't always work together. I'm on crime squad. Tai's on break. That means breaking and entering."

Tanea nodded absently, eyes fastened on Tai. Warm. Inviting. The little minx, thought Steven. She knows Tai's fallen for a loop. Why can't she give him a break? Deliberately he spoke again, forcing Tanea to look at him.

"Maureen said you came up from the South Island. Were you nursing there, too?"

"Yes. But I thought I'd try the North Island for a change. Luckily there was this opening at the Hutt."

Her eyes clouded momentarily. Maureen butted in, started talking quickly about what Tanea could expect from the North Island. Steven did not know whether it was deliberate, whether it was typically Maureen, who did not like being left out of any conversation.

104

He sat back, enjoying the spectacle of Tai being hypnotised by this exquisite creature. Finally, it was time for them to leave. Tai jumped up, gallantly offered to escort them home. Maureen pointed out it was only a few doors along the street but Tai insisted. Laughing, they waved goodbye, Tai in the middle, arms linked with those of the two girls.

"Well, what d'you think of her?" Kylie asked when they closed the door and she set about clearing the table.

"Very nice. And it seems Tai thinks so, too. Maureen doesn't need to introduce her to anyone else. I think Tai has plans of his own."

Kylie looked at him frowning. "I didn't mean that. Of course, it's nice she's met someone like Tai. He's a fine boy and he'll be good for her but—"

She stood there, hands on hips, glaring at him. "You don't even know who she is, do you?" she challenged.

Steven was puzzled. "Should I?"

"Oh, you men!" said Kylie impatiently. "Don't you remember? She's that girl Maureen told us about."

Steven stared at her, searching through his memory trying to pinpoint the particular item he should have remembered. Maureen was always chattering about someone, something, so much so that Steven had adopted a self-defence system of not really listening. There was something. Something about a psychiatric nurse.

He swung on Kylie. "You mean, she's the one who found the suicide?"

"Yes, that's right. Had a pretty rough time for a while."

"Poor kid," said Steven. "Must've been a helluva shock. But she seems to have got over it all right."

"Yes, thank goodness," said Kylie placidly. "And Tai will help. I think Tai will be very good for her."

She turned on the tap, began to wash the dishes. Steven picked up the tea towel, helped her to dry. He had been right. Kylie had brought Tanea back purely to meet Tai. That explained her matchmaking look. Poor old Tai! He never had a chance.

CHAPTER XI

ON FRIDAY MORNING Steven had time for a brief discussion with Charlie Fenton before Peacock arrived. Once again he asked permission to make the inquiry official. Peacock grunted, fingering the carefully-worded report.

"Semi-official maybe. Once it's official we have to notify Nelson. And what can we tell them? Nothing really. Not enough in this hodge-podge to make it worthwhile. Not enough solid facts. Too much speculation." He sighed. "Right. You can contact Auckland and Gisborne on those points. See what they have to say. Anything supporting your theory, we'll have another look at it."

The telephone rang. Peacock answered it, expressed surprise, said, "Yes. Of course. Ten minutes. Certainly we'll be here."

He cradled the receiver, looked at Steven, frowning. "Marshall Thorpe. Wants to consult us with regard to the Ancell affair. A client involved, he says. What d'you think?"

Steven shook his head. He had no idea, no idea at all. Marshall Thorpe, QC, top man in his field, too important to be running errands for anyone. Anyone? He had enough prestige to command their presence yet he was coming to see them. That had to mean he had a favour to ask. A favour? What kind of favour would a man like that have to ask?

Hurriedly, Steven made out one telex for Auckland, one for Gisborne, had barely time to arrange their sending before Marshall Thorpe arrived.

His overpowering presence filled the small room, heavy black eyebrows over brooding eyes, mane of white hair neatly waved around the square-jawed face, heavy frame of a former All Black. Usually he was curt, impatient, with police personnel. This morning he was smiling, honey-voiced. Definitely seeking a favour.

He raised his eyebrows at Steven's inclusion but made no demur, seated himself in the chair indicated, placed on the desk a large manilla envelope he carried.

"You have information in regard to the Ancell case," said Peacock.

Thorpe seemed shocked by this abrupt start of the meeting, entered straight away into Peacock's ploy. "Perhaps, Chief Inspector. Actually, I'm seeking information from you. On behalf of a client whose identity I cannot divulge. If you're prepared to help me—my client—maybe we can help you."

Peacock looked at him dourly, considered. At last he said with a show of reluctance, "Your client would not be criminally involved in the Ancell case?"

"No. No. Quite the contrary. Purely an innocent and completely accidental contact, I assure you."

Peacock grunted. "All right. Tell me about it."

Thorpe hesitated this time, hedging. "First, I must outline what I know of the Ancell case. Carter Ancell disturbed a burglar in the act of robbing his safe and was killed. Correct?"

"More or less."

Thorpe fiddled with the metal fastening on the envelope.

"I understand the safe is situated in a workroom at the back of the shop where Mr Ancell did minor repairs. Can you tell me if everything was taken from the safe?"

Peacock shook his head. "No. Only certain items were taken. Mostly fashion jewellery of the medium price range."

"Ah! Then perhaps you can let me have a look at what is left." Thorpe waited but Peacock remained silent. "Come along, man, I simply wish to ascertain whether a particular piece of jewellery is still there. My client left it with Mr Ancell on Monday."

"I see. Then perhaps you could describe the piece to us. We know exactly what was left."

"Well, putting it broadly, it's a brooch. Nothing pretentious. Entwined gold stems with a—gem inset."

Peacock shook his head. "All the brooches were taken. If the brooch was in the safe that night, it's gone, I'm sorry to say."

Thorpe sighed. "I was afraid of that." He looked out of the window at the blazing sky, tapping his fingers lightly on the desk. "Yes, I was afraid of that."

"All right," said Peacock. "Let's stop playing games. Tell us about the brooch. How it got into the safe."

Thorpe brought his eyes back to Peacock's face. "Before I explain all that, I must have your absolute assurance that nothing of this conversation will be divulged to the press. In fact, to anyone outside this room."

107

"You have our absolute assurance," said Peacock quietly. "As a matter of fact, if this brooch is valuable—and I gather from your comments it is—then we will most definitely keep that information quiet. Y'see, this thief we're talking about steals only mass-produced stuff that can't be identified. If he's saddled himself with an identifiable item—and we can locate it—we have an open and shut case. It's in our own interests to keep quiet."

The big man nodded gravely. "Well, I have to advise you that my client is a lady who was born in New Zealand. She went overseas, made an extremely wealthy marriage. She and her husband are at present visiting the country. In fact, they are staying at the old homestead on the Wainui coast. Naturally, my client was intrigued by all the progress in the valley. It's been considerably built over since she was last here—well over ten years ago. No shopping Mall even—just plans at that stage. On Monday she drove the small car down, had a roam around the Mall. By herself. She did not expect to meet anyone she knew but, as it happened, she did. Carter Ancell. While she was talking with him in his shop, the clasp of her brooch came undone. It is faulty. Carter Ancell offered to fix it for her if she would leave it with him overnight. Well, she didn't want to hurt his feelings so she gave it to him. Carter Ancell placed the brooch in a small box like this one."

He undid the metal fastening of the envelope, fished out a brooch box, opened it. "Also my client says this brooch here is similar to her own in design. The materials are inferior, of course, but to the casual eye they are more or less identical. An unpretentious piece, as you see, even though it is so valuable."

It was a Delacourt box, Steven noted, white outside, scarlet inside. The brooch was a pretzel of gold wire with a thumbnail teardrop in blue.

"There are other differences, of course," continued Thorpe. He brought out from the envelope a velvet case, opened it on the desk. "Here are matching earrings—" Little florets of gold with blue centres. "And this chain—" He picked out a delicate tracery in fine gold, held it up for them to see. "The centre piece of the brooch is meant to be worn as a pendant. There's a small knob of gold which you press. The stone and immediate gold surround detaches from the rest of the brooch, is then attached to this chain."

Steven helped himself to one of the earrings, held it to the light. Inside the blue depths a star was born. Star sapphires? Beside the real thing the paste replica seemed glassy and brash yet, a few moments before, it had seemed extremely attractive.

He turned the earring over. On the smooth back of the mount was stamped the designer's mark, a double asterisk. Steven realised Thorpe had his hand out, gave him the earring.

"Well, gentlemen, I'll leave this brooch with you. Watch out for something like it. It might be the brooch I'm looking for." He replaced the earring and chain in the velvet box, put that inside the envelope, refastened the metal clip. "I do hope you will be able to trace the real brooch for my client."

Peacock accepted the Delacourt box, looked at the imitation brooch nestling in its scarlet satin, snapped the lid shut.

"Thank you very much for coming in, Mr Thorpe. This could be most helpful. Just what we wanted. An identifiable object. In fact, I think you can tell the Baroness we are quite hopeful."

Thorpe turned a delicate shade of puce. Peacock smiled.

"We are policemen, sir, and you did give us some obvious clues. It could only be Baroness van der Muhll. We all know she's in the country. We know she's staying at the family homestead."

Thorpe hurrumphed a bit, suddenly laughed heartily. "Touché. But you could've remained diplomatically uninformed until I was actually out of the room," he said. "However, no harm done. And now you know why we don't want any publicity."

Chuckling to himself, he left the room, his task accomplished.

After the door closed, Peacock leaned back in his chair. "Well, at least now we know why Carter Ancell went back to the shop. That's something. If we can locate that brooch, pendant, what have you, we've got our man."

"The operative word being 'if'," warned Steven.

"Yes. Unfortunately it could be hiding right now at the bottom of somebody's jewellery box." He stopped, rubbed his chin thoughtfully. "What about Judy Lismore? I didn't want to go over to Wainui today but it looks as though we have to."

"Why Judy Lismore?"

"Why not? We've searched Carter Ancell's house. Luke's flat. Judy Lismore seems to be our next best possibility."

Steven could not argue with that.

They went down together to obtain a car, set off for Wainui. Steven kept thinking of Judy and Luke all the time he was driving up and over the hill, down through the valley to Judy Lismore's modest home, only six streets away from the fire-blackened hill.

She seemed surprised to see them when she answered the door, invited them in without any show of concern. Peacock first went

109

over her previous testimony covering Monday night. When it seemed he was satisfied, he came to the purpose of his visit.

"I'm sorry, Mrs Lismore, but we'd like to have a look at your jewellery, if we may."

"My jewellery?" She looked from one to the other. "But I haven't much in the way of real jewellery. Just costume stuff."

"Most of which Luke gave to you?"

She flushed. "Yes. Of course. He's in the business." Her voice trailed, sharpened. "Are you trying to suggest Luke stole them? From Uncle Carter? You're quite mistaken. I know everything's been paid for. Come this way, gentlemen."

Her voice was icy, eyes hostile as she led the way into the cream and gold bedroom. "There!" she said, pointing a peremptory finger at the low dressing table. "The top drawer."

Peacock opened the narrow drawer, quite unabashed. The items it contained were similar to the more expensive range offered for sale at Ancell's Gifts and Novelties. Peacock lifted out the pieces, examined them in silence, replaced them in the drawer.

"Are these all you have?" he asked quietly.

"Yes, that's—" she had started to say waspishly when she stopped abruptly, eyes darting towards the wardrobe door.

"You've got some more in there, have you?" Peacock said, moving over to the built-in wardrobe. He made no attempt to open the door, simply stood there waiting for her to do it for him.

Judy walked over reluctantly, opened the door, reached up to the top shelf, lifted down a clear plastic bag containing about twenty little white boxes, handed it to Peacock. Peacock lifted it up to scrutinise the contents, smiled bleakly.

"When did Luke give you these?" he asked.

"He didn't give them to me. I'm just minding them while he's away on trips. He couldn't very well leave them at the flat."

"You still haven't told me when he gave them to you."

Judy hesitated, said coldly, "When he started travelling for Wright's. About three weeks ago."

"You're sure?"

"Of course I'm sure." Her eyes were bright. Steven had a feeling she might break into tears any moment now. Only her fierce pride was preventing it.

Peacock offered the bag to Steven. "Recognise any of these?"

Steven dipped in his hand, opened three of the white boxes with their scarlet linings. "Yes. They are similar to the ones on that last order."

Peacock nodded, watching Judy closely. There had been no reaction to Steven's statement, only dull acceptance.

"We'll have to take these, I'm afraid, Mrs Lismore. We'll give you a receipt and you may get them back eventually."

"Take them and be damned!" Judy flared. She turned her back on them determined they should not see her crying.

Peacock nodded. They left the room, the house with its green lawns and pebble gardens. In the car, Steven went methodically through the little boxes, recognising most of the trinkets. There was no sign of the star sapphire brooch.

"I thought it was too easy," he sighed, placing the bag on the seat beside him. "What now?"

"Now we see Luke Ancell."

They went on down the main road, parked the car in front of the base, spoke a few words to Driscoll who came hurrying out to meet them, walked over to the Mall.

There were crowds of shoppers, busy, busy. Some looked at them curiously as they walked through with the plastic bag rolled into a neat bundle. Fortunately, there were no customers in Ancell's Gifts and Novelties. Peacock and Steven entered, looked around at the glittering display.

"In here, Inspector," Luke called sharply. "I sent Mrs Martin out for a message."

They walked down to the office with its one-way glass, found Luke with some of the company books on the bench in front of him. He did not even glance at them, presenting a flawless un-friendly profile.

"Just looking up the information you need to cover those things you lifted from Judy," he said crisply. Hostile. Aloof.

"She rang you?" Peacock's voice was mildly inquiring.

"Sure. What did you expect? Of course she rang me. Straight away. Now she knows what I meant by getting involved. I knew you'd start pushing her around sooner or later. A woman! Easier to upset, eh?" The blue eyes were filled with contempt.

"We're operating on information received," grated Peacock.

"So you say. Anyway, those bits and pieces were bought and paid for before I left the shop." He placed papers, books in front of Peacock. "See this. That's the order placed by me. These are Delacourt's invoices. Here's the record of my payment to Uncle Car." His finger stabbed angrily at the appropriate entry in the cash book. "So where does that leave you!"

Peacock refused to be drawn. Slowly, he examined the order

form and the accompanying invoices both dated January.

"This order is for forty items. There's only twenty odd in this bag. Where are the rest?"

"I've sold them, of course. Anything odd about that? That's what I got them for—to sell. I thought if Uncle Car held out too long I'd go into business myself. In a small way."

"May we have a look at the order covering the goods that were stolen?" Blandly.

Luke opened the order file, lifted out the copy. Peacock placed it beside Luke's order, studied them both.

"I notice this order of yours covers practically the same items as your uncle's order. Everything on your order also appears on his order."

"Good lines. That's why I picked them. I've learned something while working for Uncle Car, y'know."

"Have you any way you can identify the items in this bag as being the ones you personally received from Delacourt's?"

Luke frowned. "Why, no! They're mass-produced. Might be some differences but nothing—" He stopped, looked at Peacock, eyes narrowed. "Hey, what're you getting at?"

"Simply that you cannot positively identify these. You admit it yourself. Therefore you cannot likewise prove they are *not* the ones taken from the safe on Monday night. As far as we are concerned, we believe these are the ones taken from the safe. That's what we're getting at." Smoothly. Unctuously. The trap baited and sprung.

Luke stared at him in disbelief, eyes calling Peacock names, pungent names, but apparently he realised it was wiser not to give vent to his feelings.

Finally he gained control, shook his head, said quietly, "You'd never be able to prove that one, Inspector. Never. I can produce people, papers, to show I bought that stuff over a month ago. Judy will swear I gave them to her—"

"Not a reliable witness," said Peacock brusquely. "Could be shown she would say anything you told her to."

Luke was silent a moment, then his lips twisted. He gazed at Peacock, mockingly insolent. "Aren't you supposed to warn me or something, Inspector? Something about everything I say will be taken down and used as evidence against me?"

"I'm not arresting you—yet. But I'll keep it in mind."

Peacock turned on his heel, left Luke staring at the wall in front of him. Steven followed at a discreet distance. He knew Peacock was angry, angry at himself for showing his hand, angry with Luke for not allowing himself to be rattled. Luke was fairly safe and he knew it. Showed it. The evidence they held against him was mostly circumstantial, could not justify an arrest, especially as Luke had a credible answer to any accusation they could throw at him.

If only they could find someone who could prove Luke's car was not outside Carter Ancell's house that night—at that time. If only they could find the sapphire brooch.

By the time they reached the short drive leading to the patrol base, Steven felt it was reasonably safe to make a comment.

"The onus would be on us to prove those pieces are the ones taken from the safe," he said drily.

"Don't I know it," said Peacock wearily. "But it won't hurt that young upstart to have a few sleepless nights."

They looked up as Driscoll appeared at the door, leaped down the steps, almost ran towards them.

"A message for you, Sergeant." He held out a piece of paper.

Steven took it, read it, handed it to Peacock. It stated briefly that Lower Hutt had received a telex from Gisborne: HETA MAIRANGI DIED CAR FIRE OCTOBER 3.

CHAPTER XII

PEACOCK QUICKLY INSTRUCTED Driscoll to advise Lower Hutt they were on their way back. He wanted to discuss developments with Rex Wiseman and Tai Bennett.

They drove in silence, Jonas chewing thoughtfully on a wad of gum, nursing the plastic bag of Delacourt jewellery. Neither of them took too much notice of the traffic, the road works, the harbour spread out like a sapphire cloak under the yellow sun. By the time they arrived back at headquarters the reply from Auckland had been received.

STAR FIVE MINOR INFRINGEMENTS INDIVIDUALS FINED SPEEDING DRUNK DISORDERLY JANUARY LAST YEAR PRELIM GANG RAPE DISMISSED IDENT NOT POSITIVE REPEAT NOT POSITIVE LEADER DIED JULY 12 EXPOSURE GANG SUBSEQUENTLY BROKE UP NO FURTHER INFORMATION.

Nothing unexpected. Even the rape charge had been anticipated. The unsuccessful charge. Gang rape required a full jury trial before the High Court. Prior to that, depositions would be heard in the lower court to determine whether prosecution had a case. In this instance, the preliminary hearing had failed.

Peacock snorted as he read the communication. "Tell them we want more precise facts. Plaintiff's name. How not positive? What do they mean by exposure? Doesn't give us a thing. Tell them to get their fingers out. Give us the information we asked for. And fast. If anyone wants me, I'll be with Wiseman."

Steven sent the telex to Auckland, had hardly returned to the office when Tai came in, a fat envelope in his hand.

"Just arrived from Wellington. For you," he said, handing it to Steven. "What gives? The boss said there's been some new developments."

Steven brought him up to date, giving him the flimsies from Auckland and Gisborne, opened the envelope. It contained photostats of statements taken during the inquiries into the incident at

the Williams Building. Steven read them carefully, passing each
one to Tai as he finished.

The first one covered the security guard, Vernon Grafton Wilson.
He stated that, in the course of his rounds, he heard the sound of
stealthy movements on the sixth floor, found the door to the outer
office of Raynor and Fleming had been forced. He pushed it open
wider. There was no sign of anyone in the outer office but the
inner office where the safe was had the door half open. He crept
over, looked through to see a man in front of the safe. He shut the
door quickly, locked it, used the telephone in the outer office to
call the police. While telephoning, he heard the sound of glass
smashing in the next room. It was loud enough for the officer at
the other end to hear. He asked what it was. Wilson told the officer
it sounded like a window breaking. He was told to leave the door
of the inner office locked until police arrived. This he did. When
the door was opened it was found the man had disappeared. A
window in the outer wall had been smashed. A small desk was
missing, the brochures and industrial magazines usually kept on
the desk strewn around the floor.

Sergeant Charles Everly Fenton reported that as a result of information received at 3 a.m. on November 18, he had a police
cordon placed around the Williams Building. He found the security
guard waiting for him in the outer office of Raynor and Fleming
as instructed. He personally unlocked the door to the inner office.
There was no one in this office but one of the windows on the outside wall was smashed. He leaned out of the window, saw the body
of the deceased on the asphalt area in front of the building. It was
dark but PC Parker was illuminating the body with his torch.
Fenton left the security guard, made his way down to the ground
floor, out on to the asphalt apron, examined the body. Beside
and partly beneath the body were the remains of a small desk
which had probably been used to smash the window on the sixth
floor.

Police Constable Dennis Tunnicliffe Parker stated he was one
of the men told off to make a cordon around the building at 3 a.m.
on November 18. He approached from the Lambton Quay side,
walking down the lane by the bank building. While crossing the
clear space between the back of the bank and the front of the
Williams Building he found the body of the deceased lying partly
over a smashed desk. The desk had splintered on impact, one of
the shards of wood being driven through the body of the deceased.
There was a considerable amount of blood on and around the

body, particularly the head which was badly damaged. The deceased was wearing gloves, was quite dead when found. Parker waited there till Sergeant Fenton came down from the sixth floor.

The medical report confirmed that head injuries received from the fall to the tarseal were sufficient to cause immediate death. A contributing factor was a heavy splinter of wood impaling the body and rupturing vital internal organs. Judging by the areas of broken bones the deceased had either dived out of the window or tripped as he leaped forward.

In the light of this evidence, the security guard was questioned more closely—to make sure Jones had not been bludgeoned to death, and his body then tossed out of the window. Wilson had been employed as security guard for less than three months. He had excellent references. His background had been thoroughly investigated by the company as was the usual custom. He was forty-eight, had a slight limp and a minor muscle impairment on his left arm, the aftermath of a car accident but, as the work was merely routine, this was not considered an impediment to the job. However, this minor disability supported Wilson's declaration that at no time would he seek to mix it with any intruder. Wilson had since left the company's employ.

Steven waited till Tai had read the last page, folded the papers, replaced them in the envelope which he put on Peacock's desk.

He and Tai discussed the statements. They agreed this new information supported their earlier belief that Jones had not been familiar with the building. No one trying to escape would jump from, let alone dive through a window on the sixth floor of any building. He would know there was no chance of avoiding injury and subsequent capture. It would be more intelligent to stay and submit quietly. On the other hand, if Jones believed he was on the ground floor, naturally he would take the chance.

Jones had lived at Otaki. That suggested he could have been unfamiliar with Wellington, might not have known of the vagaries of the Williams Building. There could even be Wellington-domiciled people who would not know about it. They would know the Terrace East was about eighty feet above Lambton Quay, might not know which buildings were affected.

Someone else knew about the building though. Someone had done the reconnoitring, had given Kara Jones reason to believe there was a rich haul to be taken from the offices of Raynor and Fleming.

The same someone who had scouted out the Rutherford Hotel for Cody Pyke? The possibility offered interesting speculation.

The telephone rang. Charlie Fenton said, "Hi there. How did my stats go? Get anything out of them?"

"And then some! Gave us the whole picture. Thanks for sending them. But one or two questions. First, what was Jones after?"

"Can't figure. Raynor and Fleming are company agents. Collect masses of dough on behalf of different people. But—and they were very emphatic about this—every bit is banked on day of receipt. Without fail. No monies ever left in the safe overnight. Anyway, be cheques mostly. Hardly the kind of loot Jones would be after. Either he got his info screwed up or he was in the wrong office."

"I see. How did he get in? D'you know?"

"Nope. Best theory to date—he came in during the day. Hid out until ready to make his hit. Happens."

It happened. The last man who did that hid in the store's locker room until after closing time, helped himself to clocks, watches to the value of $13,000. To make his escape he forced a padlocked door, thus breaking the alarm circuit and alerting the local station.

"All right. So much for Kara Jones," said Steven. "Another job you can do for us if you're interested. Go along to the Justice Department, will you. Get details of coroner's reports on a couple of deaths. One—Adam Curry, Auckland, July 12. Two—Heta Mairangi, Gisborne, October 3."

"Will do," said Fenton. "Any connection with Kara Jones?"

"Yeh. All belonged to the same bikie gang in Auckland. Called themselves the Star Five."

"The Star Five? Never heard of them."

"No. Imitators from all accounts. Grabbing a bit of the reflected glory from the bad guys."

"Oh, that kind! Harmless mostly."

"Mostly," said Steven. He replaced the receiver, looked at Tai. "Kara Jones came from Otaki. D'you know anyone up there who could make some friendly inquiries for us?"

"Sure. My cousin—Reitu Love. Owns a service station. Knows everyone. Bet he could get information out of Jones's friends without letting them realise what it is all about."

"Good. Now what about Gisborne? Any relations up that way?"

Tai laughed. "Not even ten times removed. But if you want a name, try Anton Puklowski. With the probation office. A good guy."

Peacock came back from his conference with Wiseman in a bad mood. "Definitely not Cheapskate, he says. Too many differences. First time anyone been harmed. First time for a Mall. First time only *part* of the medium-priced stock taken. Cheapskate's usual pattern's a lock-up shop on a back street. Everything in that price range gone. So not him. Wiseman says an inside job. Someone who knew about the safe key. Knew about Cheapskate. Used him for cover. Which means Luke Ancell or Hugo Benson. Don't like either of them. Just has to be Cheapskate!"

Steven looked at him in surprise. Only yesterday they were hoping it was not Cheapskate.

"Why does it have to be Cheapskate?" he asked.

Peacock smiled bleakly. "Needs to be—if the Baroness wants her bauble back. Hugo Benson now. If he took the stuff as cover he'd have disposed of it but fast. Dumped it in the river. The sea. Whatever. Luke—well, possible he spotted the sapphire brooch wasn't a Delacourt item. Discarded it likewise. Whereas Cheapskate! Skitey enough to think he's untouchable. So, one—he'll get rid of that particular haul pronto. Two—he'll hang on to it until well after the initial hoo-ha has died down, then sell. Either way he'll sell some time. Bet my bottom dollar on that!"

Steven was silent. He agreed with Peacock but—

The existence of the sapphire brooch certainly made the prospect of tagging Cheapskate with the Carter Ancell murder more practicable. But how to find him? Where did he sell his loot? Any thief had to have an outlet, some way he could offload without too much trouble. No fence would be bothered with such low-value stuff so Cheapskate had to have his own means of distribution.

A company representative as Rob Henshawe had suggested? That meant casual sales to anyone, anywhere. Hard to trace. Likewise the roving bar room supersalesman in bargain trinkets. A small shopkeeper? Delacourt would not be too happy, but they might have to make use of his company's invoices after all.

Not yet though. Perhaps in a month's time—if the Ancell case was still unsolved. Publicity would be their weapon. The media would be saturated with photographs of the brooch Marshall Thorpe had given them. Anyone who had bought a similar brooch in the last four weeks would be requested to contact the nearest police.

There was a slim chance someone might come forward. The main flaw in that scheme was that it would alert Cheapskate, perhaps sending him under cover for ever.

Still, that was all in the future. Steven settled down to the fresh reports. Tai wandered back to the break squad office. Jonas read through the photostats from Wellington, put them aside without comment, pulled the Ancell file towards him, turned some of the papers over, sat for long periods chewing gum, unblinking eyes staring straight ahead.

David Galt dropped in to report on the inquest, open and shut as was expected. Both Luke Ancell and Hugo Benson had been present. They had not seemed too friendly, had returned to Wainui in separate cars. No one seemed to know whether it meant anything or nothing.

At four o'clock the answer came from Auckland: FOR FURTHER INFORMATION STAR FIVE CONTACT DS HECTOR DUNN TRANSFERRED PORIRUA JUNE HE HANDLED.

Porirua. That was more like it. Porirua was a growing city on the west coast. Steven rang Sergeant Dunn, found he was in Wellington, left a message for him to ring when he returned.

As soon as he hung up, the telephone rang again. This time it was Charlie Fenton. "What d'you want to know?" he asked jovially. "I've taken a gander at those two coroner's reports, so you tell me what you want. I'll give."

"An outline of what happened, that's all. And the findings."

"Right. Here goes. Adam Curry. Attended party at beach house they rented. About thirty people present. Quite a shindig. Shortly after twelve went for a burn-up on his bike. With one of the females. Did not return. Next day, Sunday, a patrol spotted his bike pushed into the bushes on the side of the road. This was about 2.30 p.m. Officer investigated. Found bike in damaged condition. Front tyre blown. Wheel buckled. Relayed information back to headquarters who took over from there. That's when it was discovered Curry was—well, missing. So they began a square search around the area where the bike was."

Fenton paused. "Took them quite a while, they said, but eventually they found him. Under a fivefinger about a hundred yards in from the road. Dead, of course."

"Of course. Why wasn't the bike noticed before?"

"Road not much used except at peak hours. Commuters. Y'know. Homes in quiet beach town. Jobs in mainstream Auckland. The only access road. Goes through thick bush. Not exactly lit up like a Christmas tree either. Besides, it rained that night. Started just after midnight. Heavy stuff. Visibility practically nil. Lifted slightly around noon. That's what killed him, doc said. Exposure. Got sopping wet, then temperature dropped to near freezing. Sure he went

119

into the thicker bush for shelter, but no protection from the cold."

"No marks on him?"

"Sure. Contusions. Bruising on the shoulder. Crack on the head. Consistent with damage sustained from a fall from his bike. Probably concussed. At least, that's the theory. Explains why he wandered into the bush like that. D'you get the picture? He has a prang, gets up half-dopey from the crack on his head, no traffic on the road and raining like hell. Pushes the bike into a bush, goes in further to where the trees are thicker, curls up under the fivefinger and conks out. Mistake. Sure, nobody uses the road much winter time but if he'd only stayed at the road's edge, he might've been noticed earlier."

"You said a crack on his head. What about his helmet?"

"First thing they looked for. Then they asked around. Some of the guys swore he was wearing it when he took off but they found it later in the shed where they kept their gear."

"What did the girl say?"

"The girl? Oh, the one he went riding with. Didn't say anything. For why? Nobody knew who she was. Where she lived. Seems they ran out of booze early. Curry went down to the local for supplies just before closing. Brought this dame back."

"On his bike!"

"No. No. Took one of the cars. Belonged to a guy named Dixon. Dixon didn't go with him by the way. Someone else maybe. No one too sure. Possible he went alone. Not important anyway. Brought this dame back. Introduced her around as Eve. Tallish. Slim. Good figure. Black shoulder-length hair. Eyes grey—green—hazel. Take your pick. Heavy make-up. Guys said around twenty-five. Girls said more like thirty-five. That's why the heavy make-up. Girls also said clothes pretty pricey. So, probably some well-heeled female getting her kicks out of slumming it with the gangs. Anyway they never traced her. Advertised but no response."

"Anybody ever seen her with Curry before?"

"Nope. Just a casual pick-up from all accounts. But Curry quite taken with her. Showing off and all the rest of it. Couldn't move fast enough when she suggested a burn-up on his bike."

"She suggested it?"

"So they say. Make any difference?"

"Don't suppose so. And Mairangi?"

"Yeh, well, Mairangi. Slightly different. A party again but no gadding around on a bike like Curry. Oh, I forgot to mention. Curry didn't soak it up like the others. Supplied all the grog but kept off

120

it himself. A couple of beers—no more. Like he was rationing himself. Really temperate guy. Mairangi, now, he got stoned. Flat out. So a couple of cobbers carted him home. Names—ah, ah, yes, here they are. Ranginui Anania, John Grayson. Anyway they took him home. Left him to sleep it off in his car. An old Hillman. Car kept in a shed-cum-garage about fifty yards from the house. House in semi-rural area. Small mixed farm, y'know. Fair way from nearest neighbour. The old man a bit of a martinet. Locked the door at midnight so they all knew better than to knock him up after that. Anyway, some time during the small wee hours the car went up in flames. Electrical fault."

"They're sure of that?"

"Sure as anyone can be. Besides, evidence showed Mairangi was having trouble with the car. Electrical trouble. Just got it back from the menders after a smash. Not too happy about it. Said every time he used the indicator it blew a fuse. Suggests an electrical fault to me. Just a matter of time before the car went up in flames of its own accord."

"Any chance he was dead before the fire?"

"No show. Definite he died after fire started. Presence of carbon monoxide and soot in the body indicate. Any good?"

"No good. Everything's been explained away."

"You wanted something different?"

"Hoped. Still, they sound conclusive enough. A couple of ordinary garden-common deaths." Steven laughed shortly. "Coincidence, that's all. Two parties. Two deaths. Got me thinking. Oh, by the way. Anybody at both parties?"

"Can't say. Only name appearing on both transcripts—Heta Mairangi. Witness at the Curry hearing. Deceased in the other. What are you thinking, Steven? The parties a couple of hundred miles apart. Hardly likely they'd be the same crowd."

"No, I suppose not. Guess I'm clutching at straws."

He thanked Fenton for his trouble, replaced the receiver. All accidents. Investigated. Explained. Yet—

He thought back to the inquiry into Cody Pyke's death. His own evidence had been dismissed as irrelevant. Mairangi's death seemed straightforward enough but there were still odd factors about Curry's death. That girl, for instance. Why hadn't she come forward? Even telephoned. Nothing as anonymous as a telephone call. And Kara Jones? Why would a man dive through a window out into the blackness of the night?

Why? Why? Too many unanswered questions. Too many. Leav-

121

ing Steven with an uneasy feeling that he had missed something. Somewhere. It was incredible that four out of the Five had died within a matter of months. So incredible that he knew he could never accept it as mere coincidence. Never—as long as he lived.

CHAPTER XIII

At six o'clock Porirua rang to advise they had located Sergeant Dunn. He would be coming out to Lower Hutt as soon as he finished his business in Wellington.

Steven wondered idly why the sergeant had not simply telephoned. Still, it was only ten minutes out of his way. Instead of turning left at the gorge road, he would continue straight along the motorway to Lower Hutt. Maybe he was taking this opportunity to acquaint himself with local personnel.

He stopped speculating when Tai came in with the information garnered by their undercover help at Otaki and Gisborne.

Friends of Kara Jones admitted they had known Kara was on a "bust", said he was doing the job with someone named Ed or Eddie. No last name. Kara liked to make out he was a tough rooster, leaked continual hints about jobs he had pulled in Auckland with some gang—unnamed.

Kara told them the gang broke up when the boss jockey died and the fuzz started asking too many questions. Kara came home then. Thought the others did, too, but he had lost touch with them until one day he met this Ed accidentally on the beach. Yeh, it would be about a fortnight before the happening in Wellington.

Seems Ed told Kara about a payroll kept overnight in this office. He had the whole dope, the way to get in, the office layout, the times the watchman made his rounds, the date the payroll would be there, the lot. It should have been a walkover. When it all came out with no mention of this Ed, they decided Kara must have tried the job by himself. Served him right for doublecrossing Ed.

No, they did not know Kara went in for safe-breaking. He had implied some of the gang he ran with in Auckland were experts. At the same time he reckoned it was more than his life was worth to talk about it. His friends thought this was so much hot air.

Kara had a reputation for lying, making out he was clever boy fooling the police. Most of it was empty boasting. Like the time he was supposed to have been pulled in for rape. Kara reckoned it happened all right but the fuzz could not touch any of the gang. They were protected by the boss man. Anyway he claimed the girl ended up on a funny farm so nobody took much notice of anything she said. His friends mentioned this in passing to show what a liar Kara was. Kara had never been in trouble with Otaki police.

The report from Gisborne told them a little more about the party Mairangi had attended on the night of his death, gave a list of the people there, detailed backgrounds of the two who had taken him home, bedded him down in the car. They seemed relatively harmless, heavy drinkers, brawlers, but mostly they kept their general cussedness inside their own crowd.

At six-thirty Peacock was summoned to the office of the commander to discuss the Ancell case. Steven watched him go with some misgivings. Unfortunately they had made too little progress to satisfy the commander.

At seven o'clock Sergeant Dunn arrived. A crisp tap of knuckles on the open door and Steven looked up to see this huge man filling the doorway.

Hard face, hard eyes, close-cropped hair, bully written all over him. Steven recognised the type—the monster tolerated at every station to frighten reluctant suspects into telling the truth.

Dunn introduced himself in a harsh grating voice, came into the room at Steven's invitation, light-footed, pantherish, seated himself on the indicated chair. Steven disliked him on sight.

"You wanted to see me about the Star Five case, the boys tell me." Voice flat, face expressionless.

"Yes. Something's cropped up. The more information we have the better. We understand you fingered them for gang rape."

Dunn shrugged. "Nothing came of it. Plaintiff didn't show. Case dismissed."

"Plaintiff's name?"

"Senga Louise Wilson."

Steven wrote that down. "Something about the identification not being positive, too, wasn't there? Can you elaborate?"

"Their defence. Kara Jones had motel bills, a tart, to prove he wasn't anywhere near Auckland that day. Ergo—if plaintiff mistaken over one identity, maybe the lot."

"And you?"

"Pack of lies. Bill made out to K. Jones. Could be Kupe Jones. Cousin. Stick together, y'know."

"You checked with the motel, of course."

"Of course. Owner remembered the dame. Did all the business. Registering. So on." Dunn's thick lips twisted.

"As for the man—well, he claimed he didn't see him much. Wouldn't identify any photographs. Didn't want to be involved. Anyway—cousins. Look-alikes. Maybe he was playing safe."

"The girl friend?"

"Kupe's woman. Ready to swear she spent the week-end with Kara out of spite. Said she'd had a row with Kupe. Oh, yeah! We reckon Kupe put her up to it. Just waiting to get her into the witness box to show what a goddamned liar she was. But the case didn't get that far."

"Why didn't your own witness turn up?"

"Had enough, I guess. Y'know the drill. Questions. Questions. And more questions. We all had a go. All of us. And she had a fair idea what it would be like at the hearing. What they'd do to prove their clients' innocence. Court gave us an hour to produce her. We tried—but couldn't talk her into it. Anyway, be dynamite to get her to testify the state she was in."

"What state exactly?"

"Shaking. Half-crying. Ready to crack any minute. Just her mother being there held her together, I reckon. Fine woman, Edith Wilson. Wanted to testify against the louts herself but of course—" He spread his hands. "Anyway, we tried for another remand. Trouble was, we couldn't guarantee she'd turn up then. So defence trotted out this motel stuff and that was that."

"You interrogated Senga Wilson?"

"Yeh. I put her through the hoop. Y'know."

Steven knew. The brutal questions, intimate, probing, stripping the victim of any shred of dignity—a necessary but unpleasant duty of the interrogating officer to weed out the ones who cried rape for some peculiar female reason of their own.

"An Auckland girl?"

"No. Worked for a travel agency. Transferred to Auckland coupla months before. Hardly settled in when this happened."

"What was she like? To look at? As a person?"

"Senga? Young. Only twenty. Tall. Slender—skinny almost. Hair like—like sunlight. Eyes as blue—" Steven looked at Dunn sharply, looked away again. The harsh planes of the man's face were softened with tenderness, eyes glowing with some inner hurt. "And frightened. Like a little child. Lost and stumbling in the dark. I don't think she'd ever been touched by dirt in her whole life. And it had to be this!"

125

He drew a deep breath. His voice lost its gentleness, resumed its normal detached harshness. "There are some people should never come up against the muck we stub our toes on every day."

Steven looked back at Dunn, the hard face, the agate eyes, the aura of brutish indifference all carefully back in place.

"D'you know where she is now?"

"No idea."

"And the Five? You lost interest in them afterwards?"

"Not quite. Kept tabs for a while. Thought they might try it again. But no—they played it cool."

Dunn leaned back indolently in his chair. "Got them for the usual stuff, of course. Assault. Disorderly. Couple of times. Didn't do much good. Got off with fines. Y'know. Couldn't touch them really. Gainfully employed. All that stuff."

"Just general harassment?"

"Yeh, I guess." Offhand. Unconcerned. Yet even he must have realised why he had been transferred from Auckland to a minor posting at Porirua.

Steven toyed with the idea of bringing him up to date, decided against it. The man had not asked any questions, merely offered answers. Perhaps he knew as much as, even more than Steven. Perhaps he did not. Could be he was no longer interested—as he inferred. Could be he had his own ideas, his own plans.

Instead, Steven picked up the list of people at the Gisborne party, placed it in front of Dunn. "D'you recognise any names?"

Dunn glanced at the list casually. "Heta Mairangi. One of the gang. Ed Perry. Not a member. A hanger-on. Good with bikes, I believe. Used to keep theirs in shape anyway. Not at the time we clobbered them for rape. After that. Some people are attracted by that sort of thing, y'know."

He sneered as he replaced the paper on Steven's desk. "Didn't run a bike himself. Had a car. Auckland could give you the details. A beat-up thing held together by wire. How he ever got a warrant of fitness—" He shrugged.

"None of the other names mean anything to you?"

"Nope. Should they?"

"Maybe not. But—" Steven stopped talking as Peacock walked in, looked inquiringly at Dunn. Steven introduced him, gave him the gist of the interview.

Peacock picked up the list, flicked it with his hand. "So Perry's the only name you recognise. We've got access to photos of the Five but Perry—you've given us a description, of course?"

Dunn said in his gravelly voice, "Not yet, sir. Just started talking about him but—well, mid-twenties, five ten, eleven. Stringy. Narrow shoulders. Hair—light brown, longish, wears it all over his face. Eyes grey. Wears glasses. Those gold-rimmed kind. Outdoor type. Skin dark-tanned like he's outside most of the time. Goatee beard. Wispy. Heavier moustache. Gingery—both of them. Reasonably tidy. Goes in for jeans, casual stuff."

"Good," said Peacock, obviously surprised at the fullness of the description. Steven had a feeling Dunn could reel off similarly-detailed descriptions of any of the Five or their companions.

"I don't suppose you know where to find him?" asked Peacock.

"No. Only address we had—same as the Five. Rented this beach house. Community living. All dubbing in. Perry just one more." He hesitated. "Are you after them, sir? Any chance you could use me?"

Peacock looked blandly from Dunn to Steven, back again, said slowly, "We are not after them, Sergeant. Just curious. Now it seems you've cleared everything up for us."

Dunn seemed disappointed, an expression quickly masked as he made his farewells. Peacock waited till the man's footsteps sounded on the stairs, turned to Steven. "What was that all about? Got a vendetta going or something?"

"I think so. Resents their getting away with it. Wants a chance to get his own back." He knew what Peacock would make of that remark. It was drummed into them all along the line—never become too involved in any case. Never. Steven kept remembering the way Dunn's face had changed when he spoke of Senga Wilson.

Peacock picked up a chair, turned its back to Steven's desk, straddled it. "Right," he said. "Get young Bennett in. This inquiry of yours. You've got twenty-four hours to resolve it or drop it. Understand?"

Steven understood. He called Tai in and together they sifted through the information they had, sorted out areas still requiring confirmation, Peacock sitting on the sidelines dropping in a word here and there.

One person seemed involved in everything. Ed Perry.

Perry had been at Mairangi's party. Dunn's information suggested he was most likely at the Auckland party also. Steven made a check sign. Jones had hinted at working with Ed while in Auckland, had talked about Ed or Eddie arranging the payroll theft. A fixer had arranged the job for Cody Pyke—someone who drove an old station-wagon type car. Ed Perry drove "a beat-up thing held together by wire" to quote Sergeant Dunn.

Dunn also claimed Perry had attached himself to the Five after the alleged blocking incident. Some people were attracted by that sort of thing, he said. But Perry? Their other points against Perry suggested he "arranged" thefts.

It all smacked of the newest trend. Crime to order. A receiver or fence gave a shopping list to a middle man. The middle man recruited his own burglars who would be instructed when and where to make a lift, where to deliver it, everything set out so they did not need to make any plans for themselves.

Was Perry such a middle man? Had he enlisted the Five to do his legwork, paying them off with cash commission, parties, even women, keeping them in line with implied threats? Curry had been head man. When he died, the rest of the gang had turned chicken, scattered to their home towns. Had that constituted a threat to the organisation? Did they know too much? Needed to be silenced?

Each death had taken place in a different police district. That meant a fresh team of investigators each time, each incident isolated from the others, nothing to draw attention to any possible connection. Until Asa Pyke began to have doubts.

Peacock nodded gravely when this theory was propounded. "Yes. It's quite on the cards Perry's a middle man as you say. Could be. Certainly explains away the tie-in. But you're forgetting Senga Wilson."

The two younger men looked at him blankly.

"Senga Wilson is also a name that links them together. Just once, of course, but look at the Williams Building break-out. The security guard was named Wilson. Remember? A definite overlap there. Jones. Perry. Wilson."

"Wilson," mused Steven. "Common enough name. Hardly likely—"

"But you don't *know*. You can't be sure. Not until you've made positive inquiries. You can't simply forget it happened."

"They investigated that one, sir!" protested Tai. "Proved that Wilson was physically incapable of handling Jones."

Peacock was silent. He looked at Tai who backtracked hastily. "Yes, I guess our first move is to eliminate that side of it. We can get her address from Auckland—"

"The flat she was renting. Just been shifted there by her office, Dunn said." Peacock tented his fingers. "Kara Jones mentioned a

128

funny farm. Give you any ideas? Like, for instance, she was committed, treated, released?"

"Committed, definitely," said Steven. "Dunn was bleeding. Guilt
symptoms everywhere. Maybe he thinks he pushed her over the
edge. Still, even if she'd been cured, she would still have to keep
in touch with the hospital. I'll get Auckland to check with Oakleigh—"

"Not just Oakleigh. She wasn't a local girl, remember? So all
of them, eh? Just in case." Peacock studied the excited grin that
had appeared on Tai's face. "All right. So you find Senga Wilson.
Eliminate her. Maybe. That leaves Ed Perry. A middle man tidying
up, you say. So what are you going to do about it?"

Steven looked at Tai, silent, frowning. Peacock sighed.

"You know you can't touch Perry. Not for accidental deaths.
That's what they are, officially. You'll need a pretty strong case to
reverse any coroner's finding. Meantime, what about Guy Dalziel?
Do you warn him or let him take his chances? Think about it."

He gave them a bleak smile, stood up, replaced the chair, left
the room. Steven watched him go, drained of emotion.

"That's telling us," he said wearily. "Maybe we are reading too
much into this. Got carried away, eh? Time enough to draw conclusions when we have a few more answers."

"Time enough!" said Tai bitterly. "What chance breaking the
case inside twenty-four hours now!"

Steven spent half an hour sending out telex inquiries to stations
located near mental hospitals, looked at the clock, decided it was
time to go home.

He was bone tired. All he wanted to do was to go to bed but
Kylie insisted he sit down to a ham salad sandwich, a steaming
mug of hot milk coffee—and conversation.

"Does that mean the Ancell case is fixed up?" she asked.

"No. We're just stumbling along on that one." Not interested.

"But usually when you stay this late it means you're winding
up. I hoped it meant you didn't have to go in tomorrow."

"I have to go in tomorrow," said Steven firmly, tackling the
sandwich without enjoying it.

"You won't be working late, will you? I mean it was supposed
to be your day off and we'd planned to go to this exhibition."

"Exhibition?" repeated Steven, wondering why his brain was
not responding to her clue.

"Yes. The Edenware exhibition. Remember? There's quite a
bit about it in the paper. Look!"

She picked up the paper, folded it so the article was uppermost, placed it on the table in front of him. It covered fully half of the "Focus" page, three photographs. Steven barely glanced at it, knowing Kylie would fill him in with the details.

"By the way, I've paid for the Petal bowl. Went up there this afternoon to make sure. Everyone was madly busy. Setting it all up. They've got some lovely stuff there, Steven, really beautiful."

She gave him his milk coffee. "Anyway, I managed to get hold of Mr Comstock. He's the president of the Hutt Art Society—the people who arranged the exhibition. And he had the list of all the pre-sold pieces including ours. So I paid him then and there—just to make sure. Of course, we have to leave it for the actual show and I promised to pick it up before the exhibition closes. Around ten o'clock, they think. That all right?"

"All right with me," mumbled Steven.

It was a pity about the exhibition. Somehow he did not think he would make it. Kylie would have to go on her own—as usual—unless she could talk one of her friends into going with her. He quickly suppressed a twinge of guilt. At least he knew Kylie would not hold it against him. A policeman's daughter, she understood how these things happened, could not be helped. To make up for it, the least he could do was to show some interest in her chatter.

"Quite a mob there. Busy as bees. Most of the art society, I imagine, and of course the Wilsons." Steven felt a faint stir of attention. He had forgotten Edenware was produced by Eden Wilson. "They had to be finished by six, Mr Comstock said. They're throwing a party tonight to introduce the Wilsons to the public. It's not just her exhibition, y'know. Her son's showing paintings, too."

"Her son?" interposed Steven, feigning interest. "Wouldn't have thought she'd have a son old enough."

"Well, she does. He's twenty-three, so that means she must be in her forties. Though I would've said younger. A lot younger. Her son's like her. Nice looking boy. Quite talented, they say. Paints landscapes. Spends his time roaming the country looking for likely scenes. Great life, eh?"

"I'd say. Does he sell much? Or does he live off mum?"

"Oh, Steven!" cried Kylie. "That wasn't necessary. It says here he hasn't been painting long. Not to sell, that is. But already he's made quite an impression. If this exhibition's a success, he's going to paint full time. Better than working from eight to five, he says."

"Oh, he did go to work then. That's nice." He sipped the coffee. "I'm sorry, Kylie. Right now I'm so bushed I couldn't care less about the Wilsons. Now if her name had been Edith instead of Eden maybe then—"

He stopped as Kylie looked at him round-eyed. "But her name is Edith. I said what a pretty name to Mr Comstock. He told me it's a trade name made up from the first two letters of her christian names—Edith Enid. Perry suggested it when she first went commercial."

Steven stiffened. "Perry? Who's Perry?"

"Peregrine. Her son. Signs all his paintings Peregrine W. Of course, most people call him Perry for short."

"My God! Do you realise what you're saying!" cried Steven. He snatched up the paper, examined the photograph. A head shot of Peregrine Wilson in front of one of his paintings. Thin face, narrow shoulders, longish hair brushed back from a high forehead. Light-coloured eyes. No glasses. No goatee beard or moustache. Steven skimmed through the interview, paused at a quote, "I still play around with engines, but now I do it only when I feel like it." He looked back for the information that had prompted that quote. Peregrine Wilson was a qualified auto-electrician.

Quickly, Steven brought out a pencil, sketched in glasses, goatee beard, moustache, brought the hair all over the face as Dunn had described. Could be! Could be! And the names! Eden Wilson. Edith Enid Wilson. Edith Wilson, the mother of Senga. Peregrine Wilson. Perry. Ed Perry.

He jumped up from the table, rushed to the telephone, bubbled his intuitive information into Peacock's receptive ear. Fifteen minutes later he replaced the receiver, waltzed back to the kitchen, picked up Kylie, carried her triumphantly off to bed.

CHAPTER XIV

SATURDAY MORNING. Three of them discussed strategy, Jonas Peacock, Steven Arrow, Tai Bennett. For the present, Guy Dalziel was safe. Perhaps he was not even in danger but that was a chance they could not take.

Last night, Lance Brendon had made a routine traffic inquiry, had found Dalziel at home playing cards with three friends—by the look of things set for a long session. Periodic checks on the house confirmed this, the friends leaving in the early hours.

Now a police car was unobtrusively guarding the area although it was not expected Dalziel would surface before midday.

As the three were finishing their planning, a telex was handed to Steven. From Christchurch, it read: SENGA LOUISE WILSON DOMICILE NELSON PATIENT SUNNYSIDE TILL SUICIDE APRIL 9.

Steven nodded. "I was afraid of something like that." The coroner's report would give them details but today was Saturday, the offices of the Justice Department closed with no chance of seeing the report before Monday.

"Wait a minute. I think I know a way," said Steven. He picked up the telephone, dialled. "Maureen? Steven here. D'you mind telling me where Tanea did her psychiatric training?"

Maureen could hardly keep the curiosity out of her voice but she answered readily enough. "Sunnyside, of course. But she finished the end of last year."

"Right. Now, d'you think you could come in to see us some time this morning? A case we're working on. I think you can help."

"Really? Well, Duncan's playing in this cricket match, Hutt Valley *versus* Wellington. I'll be dropping him off at the Hutt rec. some time after ten. Then I'm supposed to go up home. Pick up mum and dad. We're all coming back to watch the match. So before that, eh? Expect me around half past ten."

Steven thanked her, replaced the receiver. "Maureen McNair. She's coming in later. Not exactly a gossip but talks a lot. More important—people talk to her. She's friendly with a young nurse who recently finished her psychiatric training at Sunnyside. While there a patient committed suicide. The only one—so it has to be Senga."

Tai's eyes were dark with concern. "Tanea?" he asked softly.

"Yes. Tanea. I understand she took it pretty badly. That's why I thought it better to get our information from Maureen."

Steven thought about Maureen. A mindless chatterer more often than not but at times she appeared particularly level-headed. He could imagine what she would be thinking now, excited at the prospect of breaching their holy of holies, anticipating every question she could possibly dream they might ask.

They went back to their meeting, had tied up all the loose ends before Maureen was ushered into the room, inquisitive eyes roaming around the small office, taking everything in as Steven introduced her to Peacock. He settled her in a chair, asked the key question.

"Maureen, when Tanea was at Sunnyside, a patient committed suicide. Did she ever mention the name of the patient?"

Maureen frowned. "Well, not her full name. Just her first name. While she was telling me about the suicide. Awful thing. Worst of all she thought Senga was getting better—then she found her. Blood, blood, everywhere, she said. Terrible. Is that what you wanted to know? The girl's name? Oh, yes, Senga. Unusual, isn't it? But easy for me to remember. It's Agnes backwards and mum's name is Agnes. That's why I remember."

"Now, please tell us everything you know about this suicide."

Maureen's eyes widened. "D'you think I ought to? I mean, Tanea told me in strict confidence—" She looked doubtfully at Peacock's grim face, shrugged. "I guess, police. You've got a good reason, haven't you? Well, Senga and Tanea went to school together. That's why Tanea was so upset when she was brought in. I mean, Senga had been pretty, really pretty, but when she came to Sunnyside—Tanea said it was horrible. She was so withdrawn. Frightened. Couldn't bear anyone to touch her. Fought like an animal every time anyone tried to do something for her. Desperately. Tanea said it was awful. She was so—so alien. Didn't recognise anyone. All alone in her own little world. She was so bad they asked the family not to visit. At least for a while. Until they got her back to some semblance of normal behaviour."

Her eyes darted from one intent face to the other. "Tanea used to talk to Senga. About the old days when they were at school together. Sometimes she'd just sit beside her. Not touching. Senga

133

couldn't bear anyone to touch her. I told you that. But she thought—just being there. Someone she'd known before."

She sighed. "One day Senga reached out and touched Tanea. Tanea said she could have cried. But she just held Senga's hand and welcomed her back. After that, Senga seemed to improve all the time, Tanea said, but one day—one day she couldn't find Senga anywhere. She went looking, not wanting to put her on report straight away. In the end, of course, she had to and they began a systematic search."

Maureen was silent, rubbing her hands together thoughtfully. "Tanea found her—found Senga. Somehow she'd managed to get hold of a razor blade. She'd cut her wrists. Her face. She'd even tried to cut her throat but must've been too weak by then because it wasn't deep enough—not to—not to— But there was blood everywhere. Everywhere. And Tanea found her. It was a terrible shock. Tanea said all she could do was whimper and cry till someone else heard her, came along and slapped her hard to bring her back to her senses. After that, well, she didn't want to finish her term but, of course, she had to. Maybe it was better she did. Anyway she's all right now. She's fine. You saw her, Steven. You'd never guess, would you?"

"No, you'd never guess," said Steven gently. "But getting back to Senga. Why suicide when they thought she was improving?"

"There was a note. Nothing much. A scrap of paper. All it said was 'I remember'. I never told you what sent her there, did I? She was gang raped. She had just been transferred to Auckland. Did I tell you she worked for a travel agency? Anyway, being in a new place she used to explore a bit.

"She went to this beach and these filthy brutes dragged her from the car. It must've been ghastly. Five of them. Oh, God, whenever I think of it! Two of them held her while the others—" She bit her lip, spoke more calmly. "That's what Senga remembered. Perhaps it would've been better to leave her in her own little world. Because bringing her back meant she remembered. And she didn't want to remember. She waited her chance and she made sure she would never remember again."

Maureen sat back in her chair, spent. Tai turned his eyes away, a sick look on his face. Tai, the big tough cop. Steven knew he was not thinking of Senga. He was thinking of Tanea—finding the bloody heap of mutilated flesh that had been her friend. The atmosphere was so electric Steven felt he had to do something to break the tension.

134

Surprisingly, it was not necessary. Maureen suddenly leaned forward, said brightly, "Is that what you wanted to know, Steven?"

Steven smiled with relief. "It's exactly what we wanted to know, Maureen. It'll help a lot. Now, we'd be grateful if you kept this under your hat for a few days. Just a few days. Okay?"

He escorted Maureen down to her car, stood on the pavement watching her drive away, breathing deeply of the clean morning air.

A maroon car slid into the space Maureen had vacated. A voice hailed him. Steven waited while Hugo Benson climbed out of his car, came on to the footpath. He wanted to see the Chief Inspector about the Ancell case. Would it be convenient to talk to him right now?

Steven assured him it would, led the way up the stairs. Benson was silent on the short trip, wrapped in his own thoughts. Steven opened the door, ushered him into the room where Peacock sat.

"Good morning, Chief Inspector," said Benson. "I went down to the patrol base expecting to find you there but they said you were working from this office today."

Peacock stared at him. "Yes, Mr Benson. We are working from this office today. What can we do for you?"

Benson sat down, said flatly, "It's about this loan Carter Ancell made to me. I've made arrangements to have it paid off. Doing it through my lawyer, keeping everything legal and shipshape. The cheque will be made out to Carter Ancell Estate."

"I'm interested to hear that, of course, Mr Benson. But it's hardly my province. Any particular reason why you came all this way to tell me? You could've phoned."

Benson licked his lips. "It's the way things are going at the Mall, Inspector. This murder's upset everyone, of course, but some of the people out there— Been making funny remarks. About Luke naturally. About me, too. I'm not a sensitive man ordinarily but this needling— Well, to cut a long story short, I realised the information about this money I owed Carter has leaked. No, no, I'm not claiming a police leak. I know I'm not the only one Carter lent money to that way but—well, I was the only one owing when he was murdered. Somehow it's common knowledge that we'd had a bit of a barney about it. Carter and I."

He stopped, adding bitterly, "That seems to be enough motive for some people. That's why I'm letting you know I'm tidying it up. I'm letting everyone know. One way or another."

Peacock nodded soberly, "Yes, that is one unfortunate aspect of any murder, Mr Benson. I am sorry there's no way we can help at this stage."

"In other words, you don't know who did it—yet. You haven't a clue!" Scornful.

"We have several clues, Mr Benson. But none of them are coming together. You say Luke Ancell is being subjected to this as well? How is he taking it?"

"Oh, so-so. Ignoring it all mainly. But then he's been sort of low-key about everything. Keeping the shop open. Behaving as though nothing's happened. I don't get it. I always thought—" He paused, looked guiltily at Peacock.

"You always thought—" Peacock prompted.

"Well, I thought young Luke was fond of his uncle. But the way he acts. Me, I'd still be in a state of shock. I am, I guess, in a way. Even though I was never that close to Carter. But Luke! Of course, he inherits. I suppose he's just looking after his own interests really but—" He spread his hands in dismissal.

Benson left fairly quickly after planting his poison seed. Peacock looked at Steven, smiled cynically. "Seems our friend Benson's getting rattled. Things must be falling apart at the Mall. Monday we'd better do a bit of arm-twisting. Too bad it's Saturday and New Zealand's closed down for the weekend."

Steven grinned to himself. The Mall was not completely closed. Two shops had Saturday trading licences, were open till noon. Not enough. The manoeuvre Peacock suggested worked only when everyone was present, able to observe other people's reaction to persistent questioning, so they had to leave it till Monday. That meant the shoppies would have the weekend to recover their sense of fair play. Unfortunately.

So much for Carter Ancell and the Mall. Right now their efforts were concentrated on the Wilsons and what they might do.

Reports had already been received that the Edenware exhibition was attracting large and knowledgeable crowds. Both Eden Wilson and Peregrine were in attendance, signing catalogues, unobtrusively encouraging people to buy. And buy they did. More and more of the exhibits were being marked "sold"—Edenware and the land-scapes signed Peregrine W. It was going to be a successful and extremely lucrative show.

Shortly after two the surveillance car advised there was another person watching the Dalziel house—a tall, stringy man, glasses, light-brown hair, ginger moustache, tight jeans, shabby jean jacket. He was noticed on three separate occasions strolling casually in the vicinity. The stake-out had withdrawn to a discreet distance, watching the watcher instead of the house.

At three, Dalziel drove out in his Holden, turned towards the town. The watcher kept out of sight, ran to a rental car parked in a side street, followed the Holden to the local tavern.

At this stage David Galt took over the watch, following the pair into the tavern. Dalziel was playing pool while the newcomer sat at a corner table away from the main stream of customers. Eventually, Dalziel left the pool table, went up to the bar for another jug at the same time as blue-jeans was renewing his order.

The two men looked at each other in apparent surprise. Dalziel seemed delighted to see the other man. They went back to the corner table together, remained in close conversation for half an hour, heavy on the laughter, heavy on the drinking.

After the stranger left, Dalziel stayed at the pub until six when he returned home for his evening meal.

Another car followed the rental as far as Mitchell Street. It stopped outside the tennis courts where a tournament was in progress, people coming and going. Blue-jeans made straight for the pavilion, entered. The police driver followed after calling in his location, could find no sign of the jean-clad man. He later learned the keys of the rental had been left in the care of a club member by a tall, thin young man in brown slacks, brown overshirt.

Belatedly, Steven realised they should have set a constant monitor on the exhibition. This had been discussed, decided against, as they did not want anyone to notice undue police interest.

Rex Wiseman was talked into dropping in to view the display on his way home. Later he rang to tell them both the Wilsons were present, Eden Wilson giving a talk on pottery and potters, Peregrine simply standing around looking decorative in a purple kaftan.

In casual conversation with the convenor, a Mr Comstock, Wiseman learned the two Wilsons had been taking turns so there was always one on show for the benefit of the interested public. He added in a jubilant voice that he had bought himself a painting, told Steven to have a look at it when he went to the exhibition later. It was catalogue number 36, showing Mount Hikurangi against the rising sun.

Steven replaced the receiver thoughtfully. Mount Hikurangi was on the east coast, allegedly the first part of the world to be touched by the sun's rays at the beginning of each new day. Gisborne, where Mairangi had died, was also on the east coast.

At eight Steven went home, so missing the report that Dalziel had returned to the tavern, was sitting alone at a separate table as though waiting for someone.

At nine Steven and Kylie visited the Edenware exhibition. As they left their car, Steven was greeted by David, who told him Dalziel had been joined by a black-haired woman, tall, slender.

"Eve?" asked Steven.

David shrugged. "Could be. The boys say they're pretty chummy. Old friends and then some. If anything breaks I'll come to the door of the hall." He patted his pocket showing the oblong bulk of his radio.

Steven rejoined Kylie who was waiting patiently on the steps. She was used to seeing him mix an evening out with police work, made no comment as they entered the exhibition together.

About fifty people were roaming around the hall, the usual type available for hiring, reasonably large and airy, high ceiling, tall windows, curved bar counter lower right corner, doors leading to kitchen and cloaks at one end, a raised dais at the other.

The bar area had been turned into a fernery, potted plants filling that corner with green. Across the front of the stage large tubs held a profusion of summer flowers.

In the centre of the wooden floor, stepped, broken-pyramid shelving draped in gold sateen displayed the Edenware, soft blues, terracottas, stone, a sprinkling of white. The modestly-priced paintings, some twenty in all, glowed with clear crystalline light against the dark walls.

Besides the sharp-featured female selling catalogues at the table by the entrance door, Steven picked out at least six other "attendants" standing around casually.

By the fernery corner, Peregrine Wilson was the centre of a group of admirers. There was no sign of Eden Wilson.

Steven and Kylie strolled around the exhibits, enjoyed once again their own purchase—tinted swirls threading through the petalled white—moved on to the paintings.

Landscapes with a difference. A foreground object meticulously portrayed in minute detail—abandoned manmade structures decaying quietly away—but through a broken window, the tattered sail of a derelict windmill, nature spread her beauty right up to a far and distant horizon.

Wiseman's choice was slightly different. Over red and black fragments of broken brick in the foreground trailed a spray of clematis, dark glossy leaves, luminous-white star-flowers, almost three-dimensional. The rest of the canvas was awash with light—

pale blue morning sky, dark mountain shape limned with a corona of amber fire.

Extremely effective, Steven thought. A little contrived perhaps —but he gave the artist full marks. The painting was alive, magnetic, the shining radiance almost hypnotic. Momentarily he wished their own "extravagance money" would stretch to the price of a Peregrine W.

Mr Comstock paused beside them. Kylie introduced Steven and, naturally, they discussed the paintings. Apparently this was the man's pet subject. He raved about the young artist's technique: the illusion of immeasurable distances in each canvas; the use of light, always light; the attention to perspective; the subtle inference of nature's ascendancy over man; the exciting vistas of minute and ever-newly-discovered detail—

Steven managed to ask one question. "I've heard Peregrine roamed around looking for scenes to paint. D'you think he really saw Hikurangi like that—broken bricks, clematis, the lot? Or d'you think he put that in for effect?"

Comstock was shocked. "No. No. That's exactly how he saw it. Everything here is exactly how Peregrine saw the scene at time of painting. Of course, he did look especially for a front focal point that would enhance the main scenic presentation but otherwise—"

Steven smiled. Clematis bloomed in the spring, so Peregrine had to be on the east coast September/October. At Gisborne October 3rd?

He was congratulating himself on his astuteness when, over Comstock's shoulder, he saw David standing in the doorway. Making a show of consulting his watch, he excused himself, left Kylie and Comstock to continue with the conversation.

In the fernery corner, Peregrine preened and strutted in front of a new set of female devotees.

Steven found David waiting on the lower steps, walked with him to the car.

"Dalziel's left the hotel," said David crisply. "Taken the dame with him. We don't know what it's all about. But if she's Eve, maybe she's getting him some place where this Perry guy can get at him more easily."

"Yeh. If she's Eve—" It all hinged on that. The pre-arranged plan was now in operation, Tai Bennett and Matt Ruakere following in separate non-police cars, changing places occasionally so the car ahead would not notice the tail.

David and Steven did not have far to go. Dalziel had shown

139

little imagination, stopping at a recreational area between the road and river. Ordinarily on such a fine night there would have been one or two family parties making use of the barbeque pits but the fire warnings were out—no outside fires or barbeques allowed—so the place was deserted.

Tai was waiting for them this side of the ramp.

He explained that, when the blue Holden stopped, Ruakere had gone on further to a dirt road that led towards the river. From there, he was working his way through the underbrush until he was in a good position to overlook the recreational area.

"Where are they exactly?" asked Steven, taking off his jacket, folding it to leave in the car.

"Under the tallest willow." Tai pointed towards the river bank where the tender green of willows showed above the darker growth covering the low rise immediately in front of them. "Mat says a blanket and bottles so they're in for a session."

He produced a diagram showing a rough square, the river on the west, the road on the east. North was the wide strip of underbrush where Mat was now in position, south was the small hillock covered in wild lupin.

Steven tapped the circles drawn to represent the double row of poplars that screened the area from the road. "A good place for you there, David. Tai, you take this side and I'll see how close I can get along the river bank. That way we'll be watching from all four sides. Okay?"

The others agreed, David setting off along the road to the poplars, Steven and Tai half-sliding down to the hollow created by the hump in the ground. They reached the halfway point.

Tai turned to Steven, said doubtfully, "I hope we know what we're doing. I'd hate it to get around we spent the night watching a layabout getting it off with his floozie."

Steven looked at him uneasily. He kept remembering Peregrine Wilson nonchalantly basking in the admiration of his female groupies. Maybe they were over-reacting but he dare not let Tai see him wavering.

He said crisply, "You have your orders, Constable. Constant surveillance. That means you go up that bank, down the other side. You get as close as possible without letting them see you. You watch them. You keep your radio open. All the time. Until I give you the word to move. Understand?"

Tai blinked. "Yes, sir," he said smartly. "Yes, sir. I understand perfectly."

He made an abrupt right turn, started scaling the low rise, pushing through the thick lupin growth until he was out of sight. Steven continued along the track to the river.

There he paused, looked around him. It was still light, the blue-white light that came between sunset and the grey of night.

To the left, tufty grass sloped down to where the bank dropped steeply to the riverbed. To the right, young tree-daisies encroached across the path, slender stems bending under the weight of creamy flowers. Beyond was the row of willows.

Steven followed the northward track past the willows, past the largest one where Dalziel and Eve were believed to be. Another ten yards and he began to work his way back, cautiously, soundlessly, till he was able to enter the picnic area, moving through head-high tree-daisies until he was near the willow's gracefully-drooping outer branches.

Carefully he settled in one of the small clearings used by picnickers as private alcoves where they could enjoy an evening meal cooked on the barbeques provided in the cleared centre of the area. At least two alcoves from his objective was, he felt, a safe distance even if it meant he could see nothing.

None of the watchers would be able to see anything if the place Dalziel had chosen was as thickly overgrown as his. No matter. If they had guessed right, Eve was there simply to keep Dalziel occupied until Peregrine arrived.

Steven tapped his radio twice signalling he was in position. Everything was still. The only sounds were the distant swish of an occasional car on the road beyond the poplars, the evening chorus of cicadas belting out their love song.

It was too quiet. Steven knew he was close enough to hear voices if any. Uneasily he shifted position, moved forward a few feet, parted the enclosing green, found to his surprise he was looking directly at Dalziel along an opening where branches lifted or failed to meet.

Something was wrong. The pair seemed to be quarrelling. They were both sitting on the rug, Dalziel facing Steven, knees drawn up, hands hanging slack between. Eve was leaning casually on one hand, her back to Steven, clothes already showing signs of disarray.

She was offering Dalziel a bottle with dark fluid in it. Sulkily he pushed it away, full mouth pouting moodily, face half-hidden by the fall of his long hair.

Eve laughed throatily, teasingly, placed the bottle on the far side of the rug, went to work on him. She slid her fingers under

141

his shirt, pressed suggestively against him, whispered, whispered.
It had the desired effect. Dalziel brightened, flung his arms around
her, hugged her close.

Giggling, Eve leaned back, patted his cheek, kissed him lightly,
went through the whole Mata Hari bit. This time when she offered
the bottle, Dalziel took it with a grin, tipped his head back, gulped
hugely. After that, the pantomime was repeated, the skylarking,
caressing, whispering—and what about another drink, eh?

Dalziel was no match for Eve. She played him expertly: enticing
—rejecting—promising so much—giving so little. Steven had no
idea what she was constantly whispering. Whatever it was, it
worked. Dalziel was lapping it up—and the liquor.

Suddenly the play-acting was over.

Dalziel took the proffered bottle one more time, lifted it to his
mouth, took another long slug, gagged, fell forward on to his face,
the bottle spilling its contents unheeded.

Eve sat watching him, absently smoothing her dress, refastening
buttons. Gingerly she lifted his head by a long strand of hair.
There was no reaction. She let his head drop, sat there quietly,
sighed, consulted her watch, stood up, looked towards the road.

The blue-white was still in the sky, hills silhouetted dark, but
grey shadow was creeping along the valley floor, filling the hollows
with night. Cars passing beyond the poplars showed lights.

None stopped.

Eve turned, went back to Dalziel, pushed him with her toe. He
did not stir. For a moment, she stood irresolute, watching the
road, examining her fingers. At last she made her decision.

She went over to the trunk of the willow, searched around,
picked up something Steven could not define, something that glim-
mered dimly in the failing light.

A clear plastic bag, by the look of it, containing something. She
carried it in one hand, squatted down beside Dalziel, lifted his
head, began to—

"Now!" yelled Steven over the open radio. He leaped to his
feet, lunged through the intervening green.

Startled, Eve jumped up, looked once in his direction, ran
smartly the opposite way—straight into the arms of Tai Bennett.
By the time Steven reached them, Tai had the writhing, kicking
woman held firmly.

Steven lifted his hand, tugged hard at the black wig. There was
still enough light to gleam on the smooth golden braids beneath.

"Eden Wilson, I presume," he said softly.

142

The calmly-spoken words had an immediate effect. She stopped her ineffective struggling, opened her eyes, looked at him haughtily, silent and disdainful.

David called from the willows. Steven ran back, leaving Eden Wilson to Tai. As he approached, Mat sped away towards the side road.

"Where's he gone?" Steven asked.

"Bringing the car closer," said David. "Want to get this fellow up to the hospital. Quietly. Soon as possible. He'll be all right, I think. We've got the air passage free. Just hope he didn't get any mud into his lungs."

Steven looked down at Dalziel—breathing in short choking bursts—but breathing, lying on his side, face smeared with traces of mud, too drunk to know what nearly happened.

"Mud, was it?" he said musingly.

"Yes, mud." David bent down, picked up the plastic bag oozing watery mud. "River mud at a guess. From this very river. Reckon they were going to dump him on the edge of the river. Like he passed out there. Choked on the mud."

"Probably," said Steven. "The same method they used with Cody Pyke. A plastic bag filled with scraps of beech wood that time. Pulled over his head and held there. He sucked the chip fragments down into his lungs while he was gasping for breath."

He pulled out a handkerchief, masked his hand, leaned over to pick up the discarded bottle lying at the edge of the rug. Still some liquid in it—enough for analysis. He sniffed it. Liquor of some kind. Obviously not the innocuous domestic wine the label claimed it to be. No doubt laced with something stronger—a good deal stronger. Had to be, to knock Dalziel out so quickly.

But only alcohol. The Wilsons were too clever to allow anything other than alcohol to show in the autopsy. The plan would be to leave the bottle at the edge of the river where the lapping waters would wash it clean long before the body was found.

Steven searched around, found the cork, replaced it, put the bottle with the other exhibits. He looked at his watch. Nine minutes to ten. It was incredible that so much had happened in such a short time. The Edenware show was due to close at ten. Peregrine Wilson would have to wait for everything to be locked up before he could decently leave. But soon a car would be stopping beyond the poplars.

David escorted Eden Wilson back to the station while Tai and Steven waited in the gloom. Peregrine arrived at ten-seventeen.

Tai and Steven closed in on him, advised him of his mother's arrest, took him back with them, deposited him in Interview Room 2.

There was no protest, no hot denials, only stubborn withdrawn silence. As Steven said to Peacock later, it all seemed an anticlimax.

"D'you want to talk to them?" he asked.

"Not yet. I rang Nelson when Galt brought the woman in. Seems Vernon Wilson's still in Nelson. A broken ankle. Otherwise, I believe, he would've been up here taking part in this family ritual. Probably he was the one scheduled to be at the barbeque place to finish off Dalziel once Eden had lured him there. As it was, because of that cracked ankle, the other two had to make do without him. Be interesting to learn how he reacts when they tell him we've arrested his wife—and his son. So we wait to hear from Nelson first."

They waited a long time.

CHAPTER XV

WHEN THE CALL finally came through, Peacock grabbed the telephone, began to take notes in printed, space-eating symbols. He hardly spoke a word beyond a "yes" here and there, a repeat of occasional figures. As he finished each page he pushed it over to Steven who had worked with Jonas long enough to be able to read with ease the shortened-word method used by Peacock. Quickly Steven absorbed the information.

Nelson had been busy. Two men had gone out to the ten-acre section beyond the marble quarries to notify Vernon Wilson, bring him in for questioning. The father of Senga Wilson had received the news of his wife's arrest with an appearance of calm. He knew it was simply a matter of time before his son would also be in custody. The only thing left was to explain. From then on, they could not stop him talking.

Most of what he told them they already knew. He merely filled in the gaps. The family had been unhappy at the dismissal of the gang rape charge but recognised the police could go no further. They decided to see what they could do themselves.

It was a family affair, all working together. Their first action was to infiltrate the gang. Peregrine travelled to Auckland, assumed the mantle of Ed Perry. They decided Perry was a safe alias in case he happened to run into an acquaintance while in the company of one of the Star Five. He grew a beard, adopted gold-rimmed glasses and, to substantiate his identity, he transferred title of an old car he was tinkering with to Ed Perry.

After that, he obtained a matching driver's licence, set up a cheque account at an Auckland bank and he was ready. He had no difficulty in attaching himself to the gang, especially after he offered to maintain their machines. For this he was invited to live at the beach house, sharing expenses.

Peregrine soon realised the Five were not the social club they pretended to be. Adam Curry was king pin. The others obeyed

him without question. Two or three times a week Curry arranged
an expedition when they brought back TV sets, stereos and such
items, using a plain blue van which was kept for this purpose.
Curry would take charge of the loot, bring back cash which he
shared amongst them. Peregrine guessed he was a fixer, a middleman for a burglary ring. Later he confirmed this, even learning
identities of some of Curry's contacts.

The gang rape had been suggested by Curry as a copycat
initiation ceremony. The Wilsons believed it was also done to
give Curry a tighter hold on his legmen. Curry sent Kupe Jones
off for his motel weekend with instructions to bring back a receipted
bill made out to K. Jones. The block worked out exactly as
planned (as did most things Curry organised). Unfortunately for
Senga Wilson, she happened to be the girl they found by herself
that day.

Peregrine uncovered these facts, could not prove them, because
Curry always camouflaged their operations so cleverly. Then Senga
killed herself. Peregrine went home for a family conference where
they decided imprisonment, no matter how long the term, was not
enough.

Adam Curry was their first target. As usual at the parties he
put on occasionally for the Five, he stayed off the grog himself
while dishing it out to everyone else. Peregrine made certain Curry
would have to visit the local tavern that night by sidetracking some
of the supplies. When Curry brought Eve (Eden) back, he went out
to the shed where they kept their gear, fixed Curry's motorcycle.

Earlier he had constructed a small timing and explosive device
designed to blow a hole in the front tyre, the timer covering fifteen
minutes but set to operate only when the ignition was running. All
he had to do was loosen off the nut holding the front mudguard,
attach the device to the underside, tighten up the nut again and
connect a wire to the ignition system.

He came back into the beach house, signalled to Eve that all
was ready.

Around midnight, when the access road was sure to be deserted,
Eve kidded Curry into taking her for a spin on his bike—with an
invitation to spend the weekend with her. Of course when they
reached her home (eight minutes away) she found her husband
had returned unexpectedly. Eve did some fast talking, convinced
Curry she would meet him the next day, sent him back to the
party.

Peregrine waited twenty minutes before setting out after them.

146

He cruised slowly along the lonely bush road, found the damaged bike, the helmet nearby, no sign of Curry. In minutes he detached the remains of the timing device, pushed the bike into thick bush, collected the helmet.

It was not till late Sunday he learned what had happened to Curry.

Ed Perry was not one of the six people questioned by police when trying to establish what happened although his name appeared among those of persons attending the party. After all this unwelcome police interest, the Star Five became uneasy, helped along with carefully-placed remarks from Peregrine. Finally they broke up, returned to their home towns.

In August Vernon Wilson procured a job of security guard at the Williams Building—to establish his presence there in an official capacity.

At the end of September, Peregrine followed Heta Mairangi to Gisborne, renewed his acquaintance, waited around for the right moment. When Mairangi's friends left him to sleep off his drink in his car, they created the background for fixing the car to catch fire from an apparent electrical fault.

The Williams Building affair happened much as the record showed—*except* that Vernon Wilson disconnected the alarm for a few minutes so the two could enter through a loading entrance on a service lane off The Terrace. When Vernon locked the door of the inner office of Raynor and Fleming, Peregrine simulated panic, smashed the window with the small desk urging Jones to dive out quickly. The smashing of the window triggered the automatic alarm giving Vernon a good excuse for turning it off again so Peregrine, released from the office, could leave the building before police arrived. Everything else occurred as stated.

A similar pattern was used with Pyke. They chose the Rutherford because they were familiar with the hotel. Pyke had been behaving himself on returning home so when approached by Ed Perry readily agreed to keep everything secret from family and friends.

That Saturday night, Pyke went to the Rutherford as instructed, changed in the toilets, wandered around to prove to himself his outfit was accepted, went down to the car park where Peregrine had arranged to give him a masterkey. After they dumped the body in the chip pile, Peregrine went back to the Rutherford, collected Pyke's clothes from their hiding place. The only near-slip was being seen in the car park but Asa Pyke's insistence that this incident had nothing to do with his son's death took care of that.

Peacock finished his talk to Nelson with the comment, "That's bad. Very bad. Yes. I'll tell her." He cradled the receiver, looked at Steven. "Well, wraps it all up for you, doesn't it?"

"Yes. Dots all the i's. Crosses all the t's. I suppose the person I saw come up behind Cody Pyke was Mrs Wilson."

"Probably." Peacock heaved himself to his feet. "Well, come on. Let's see how Lucretia Borgia's doing."

They walked along to the first interview room, nodded to the uniform man on guard, entered. Eden Wilson paused in some small talk she was directing at her minder, a stern-faced unresponsive Peggy Taylor. The cigarette held languidly in her right hand sent a thin spiral upwards into the still air.

"Well, well, the big brass." She smiled sweetly at Peacock.

Casually she doused her cigarette, tilted her head provocatively. There was no doubt Eden Wilson was a beautiful woman. The braided hair was smoothly golden, heavy make-up wiped from her face to reveal the perfect complexion, faint age-lines around her eyes, her mouth.

Peacock ignored her flippancy, sat down, said brusquely, "Mrs Wilson, we are going to charge you with attempted murder. You are not obliged to say anything unless you wish to but anything you say will be taken down in writing and may be used in evidence."

"You mean he didn't die!" Eyes wide, brows lifted.

"Not this time. The hospital says he inhaled some of the mud. Not enough to cause permanent damage."

"What a pity!" she said. She shook out another cigarette, lit it, took a deep drag, waited, a half-smile on the lovely mouth. Peacock remained silent. At last she could stand it no longer. She pouted, said sharply, "Aren't you going to question me?"

"Quite unnecessary, Mrs Wilson," said Peacock slowly. "Four of my officers had you under observation. Nothing you can say will add to our own information."

"Except why," she snapped.

"We know why. We know all about your daughter, Senga. We've been investigating ever since Cody Pyke's death." He sighed, shifted slightly in his chair. "There is one thing I have to tell you, Mrs Wilson. Your husband is dead. A massive coronary. He'd been co-operating with Nelson police. Waiting for his statement to be typed up. A doctor was there. He had immediate attention but he died on the way to the hospital."

Eden Wilson looked at him blankly, lips stiff and white.

"You've—you've told Peregrine?" she whispered.

"No. But we'll tell him." Peacock sat there watching the woman who was suddenly not so sure of herself. She forgot the byplay with the cigarettes, forgot her critical audience, sat immobile, dry-eyed, unbending. Peacock nodded to Peggy Taylor, said, "All right. Take her away."

Peggy touched Eden Wilson gently on the shoulder. The woman turned her head inquiringly, stood up stiffly, grinding her cigarette into the ashtray. She picked up the half-empty packet, looked at it absently, dropped it back on the table, strode straight-backed to the door, waited till the door was opened for her, went through without a backward glance.

Peacock grimaced at Steven. "Bennett's with this Peregrine fellow, isn't he? Better tidy that up. Charge him. Tell him about his father."

He walked briskly from the room, Steven trailing after him, turned left while Steven went to the second interview room where Tai Bennett stood stolidly, watching the other man sitting contemptuously silent at the central table.

"Charged him yet?" Steven made no attempt to lower his voice, was pleased to note the flicker of interest in the pale eyes.

"Yes, sir. Attempted murder."

"Well, leave it right now. We've got all the information we want." Steven leaned on the table, facing Peregrine.

"I have to let you know your father died less than an hour ago."

Wilson looked at him coldly. "You're lying!" he said flatly.

Steven shook his head. "I'm not lying. He had a heart attack. After telling Nelson police all about your little capers over the last few months." He paused, said deliberately, "That's one murder you didn't plan, isn't it?"

Wilson flinched, averted his eyes.

"All right," Steven said to Tai. "Tidy up here and you can call it a day."

He left the quiet room, made his way back to the office where Peacock was reading through the information from Nelson. He looked up as Steven entered. "Quite a round-up, Sergeant. Young Bennett is to be commended. Yes, I know you thought maybe murder—but would you have done anything about it?"

Steven considered. "Perhaps. When we'd finished the Ancell case. Wouldn't have got anywhere. Timing all wrong. If Bennett hadn't started me thinking about Cody Pyke when he did, I

149

mightn't have gone to the funeral. Missed the Star Five thing. Wouldn't have made the connection with Edenware, either. And Dalziel would've been dead. No. Bennett deserves the honours. The right man at the right time. With the right connections."

Peacock nodded, cleared his desk. "Well, I'm off. And you, Sergeant, rest day for you. Come in again Monday morning. Monday we'll tear the Wainui Mall apart."

He paused in the doorway, looked back.

"Nearly forgot. Wiseman did a make on this Frank Summerfield you mentioned. Mightn't mean anything but he comes from the deep south. Dunedin. Used to work for a security firm. About three years ago."

"Interesting," commented Steven. "Very interesting."

A security man would know about burglar alarms, safes too. As Peacock said, it might not mean anything but it seemed a step in the right direction.

Steven went back to finishing off the reports he had begun while waiting to hear from Nelson. His last task before he packed up was to notify Auckland that Peregrine Wilson might be persuaded to divulge information about Adam Curry and a burglary ring.

Kylie was sound asleep when he arrived home. As he slid carefully into bed, she stirred sleepily, asked the time.

"Nearly two," he whispered. "Now go back to sleep."

"Did it all work out all right?"

"Yes. Fine. And I don't have to go in till tomorrow. Monday."

Kylie was instantly awake. "You know what that means, don't you? Aunt Tabitha. Remember?"

Steven groaned. He had forgotten about Aunt Tabitha—Great Aunt Tabitha who would be celebrating her ninetieth birthday with the whole clan summoned to pay court.

"Tell you what," said Kylie cheerfully. "We won't go till the afternoon. That'll give you a chance to have a good long sleep-in."

"Okay," said Steven, without enthusiasm. "Now go back to sleep."

They set out for the birthday celebration at 2.20 p.m.

Steven drove down from their own suburb in the western hills, north along Highway 2, turned left at the Haywards Road across the hills to reach the west coast. A mile past the electricity sub-station he saw a familiar car at the side of the road.

"Wait a moment. That's Lance. Want to see him. Mind if I

stop?" Kylie did not have much choice. He pulled in, climbed out, walked over to the black-and-white.

"Hi!" said Brendon cheerfully, opening the door. "Heard all about your shenanigans last night. Some show, eh?"

Steven laughed, settled in beside the traffic officer. They talked easily about the Wilson case while the Sunday traffic rolled past at conservative speed. Lance watched them absently as he listened to Steve, well aware that the presence of a Transport car at the side of the road was sufficient deterrent for most over-enthusiastic drivers.

"What I wanted to ask you," Steven said finally. "Remember you said you were keeping an eye on Guy Dalziel? D'you think you could turn up the details?"

"Sure. Just a matter of looking through the day books. Though what—" Lance stopped suddenly, glared at a passing car.

A cream-coloured Victor shining with loving care, it seemed to Steven to be travelling decorously enough but Lance grabbed his clipboard, flipped the top page.

"Thought so. A take. Just come in. Hot. Real hot. Stupid. Stupid." He switched on the engine, glanced at Steven. "Coming?"

"Sure I'm coming. Get weaving!" said Steven crisply, hastily fastening the seat belt. Lance tripped the siren as he sent the car surging out on to the road. The errant driver realised the siren was for him, showed his guilt by putting his foot down as hard as he could.

The Victor leaped away, passing the slower-moving cars, most of which were pulling over in deference to the siren. Fortunately traffic on the down slope was light so Lance could concentrate on the chase.

The gap between them seemed to stay constant for over half a mile, half a mile of winding road that meant they lost sight of their quarry time and time again. They dropped down to the creek, whooped over the narrow bridge, swung around the corner.

The cream Victor was straddled across the grassy verge, both front doors wide open, the driver trying to persuade his companion to leave the car. As the black-and-white came into view, he took off, dived into the cover of thick bush growing beyond the three-strand fence.

Brendon dropped all anchors, stopped within inches of the other car. Steven jumped out, raced past the stationary vehicle, barely glimpsing the white-faced girl cowering in the front seat, followed the escaping car-thief.

Once within the cool green he knew it was hopeless. The fugitive could have gone in any direction except—to the right a tangle of close-packed vines made an impenetrable wall.

Steven followed the line of the vine hedge, searching to the left amongst feathery leaves, broader, leathery foliage, spiky flax, stopped abruptly as a mallard duck whirred into squawking flight from under his feet.

He about-faced quickly, looked, listened. All around was the wall of green. Even where he had himself pushed through, branches had fallen back into place concealing any trace of his passage.

"All right," he said aloud. "You might as well give up. We've got your girl friend. She'll tell us who you are." He waited. "Come on, fella. D'you want her to take the rap by herself?"

A good ten feet away a figure materialised from behind a stunted beech thickly draped with a small-leafed creeper. Slight. Tow-headed. Young. Not a lout. Not a tearaway. Just a kid, a scared kid ready to face the consequences.

Steven said gravely, "My name is Steven Arrow. I'm a detective sergeant. What's your name?"

"Cliff Bullen," stammered the boy, moving reluctantly towards him.

"Ever been in trouble before, Cliff?"

"No, sir."

"And you start by stealing a car?"

"I didn't steal it. Just borrowed it. I meant to put it back. Fill her up with petrol again. Hardly be missed."

" But it was missed, Cliff. Reported in as stolen." He paused. "You know the owner then?"

"Yes, sir. Mr Robinson." A frown creased the young forehead. " But they weren't supposed to be coming back till tomorrow! I thought—I thought—well, it seemed safe enough."

Steven nodded thoughtfully, looking down at the apprehensive blue eyes. He turned towards the road. "All right, Cliff. Suppose you tell me all about it."

Cliff Bullen began to talk. His mother owned a tearoom and country store on the main highway between Otaki and Levin. Julie Paterson, the girl in the car, had come to stay with relations on a nearby farm. He had asked her to come for a drive, planning to use the pick-up truck belonging to the shop.

At least, that was the original idea but Julie was a town girl, probably more used to cars than an old pick-up. He began to worry about it. Then he remembered Mr Robinson's car.

Mr Robinson was a share-milker on a local farm. He lived by himself in a bach on a back paddock. On Friday night he had come into the shop, told Mrs Bullen they were going to use his friend's four-wheel drive to go into the hills after deer as soon as they had their supplies, returning Monday morning. As he left, he promised to bring Mrs Bullen a haunch of venison.

Cliff went out to the farm, found the Victor under the open-fronted leanto beside the bach. An old model but still better than a truck to take a girl joyriding. Cliff felt around on the exposed beam where he knew Mr Robinson left his keys, collected them, knew he was set to take the car. He thought if he brought it back around four, filled up with petrol, nobody would know.

By now they had reached the edge of the bush. They stepped through the fence, crossed the grassy verge to the road. Steven was not surprised to find Kylie had followed in their car, was even now soothing the weeping Julie.

Brendon looked up from examining the stolen car for damage. "Got him, eh?" he said with a smirk of satisfaction.

Cliff hurried over to Julie while Steven stopped to speak to Brendon. "What's the story, Lance? D'you know?"

"Couple of guys went out after deer. Had a good trip, bagged two good trophies, came out earlier than planned, found the car gone." He looked from Steven to Cliff, back again. "That what he told you?"

"More or less." Steven watched Cliff talking to Julie, trying to explain. A pretty child, soft fair hair, blue eyes, face swollen a little with tears. She was wearing a demure frock in ecru-coloured linen, the only ornament a golden brooch pinned high on the left shoulder.

Steven's eyes narrowed. He walked quickly over to the little group, stared at the brooch. A pretzel of gold wire set with a blue stone that shimmered into a star.

"Let's see that brooch," he said perhaps a little brusquely. He lifted his hand to have it pushed aside by an angry Cliff.

"Leave that alone. It's hers. Her mother gave it to her for her birthday. Yesterday."

Steven could tell by the break in the boy's voice that he was using anger to cover his own frustration.

"Yesterday?" repeated Steven. "Where did your mother buy it, Julie? D'you know?"

"It's got nothing to do with this!" Cliff muttered. "It's bought and paid for. Bought and paid for!"

153

"That's quite possible, Cliff," said Steven more gently. "But you see the brooch was stolen before it was sold to Julie's mother."

Cliff sagged visibly. This time there was no protest beyond a feeble, "Careful. It's got a faulty catch."

"Yes, we know about the faulty catch, Cliff," said Steven. He unpinned the brooch, lifted it away, turned it over in his hand. On the back of the gold mount was a double asterisk. He turned it back, watched the star glinting in the blue depths.

"Yes, I'm afraid this is the one. And it *is* stolen. Where did your mother buy this, Julie?"

Julie looked helplessly at Cliff, who slid his arm around her shoulder for mutual comfort. He said unhappily, "Chap comes into the shop sometimes. Company rep. Travels for Loan and Merc. Comes in quite often. Always has something extra to sell. A lot of company reps do."

"So I've heard. What's his name, Cliff?"

The boy shrugged. "Don't know. Mum calls him Chuck. She'd know his real name though, I guess."

"Chuck, eh? I know someone works with Loan and Merc. Maybe he'd know who this Chuck is. What's he like?"

As he listened to Cliff, he could almost hear the blocks clicking over in his mind—all the bits and pieces falling into place. He glanced at Brendon, an interested but silent spectator.

"Say, Lance, can I take him? I know he's your cop but it's his first so probably only probation. Right now I think he's more valuable to our side. Got information we need."

Lance thought a moment, nodded. "Okay. Your plate. You dish it out. I'll have to mention you taking the kid in my report though."

Steven grinned broadly in thanks, escorted the two youngsters to his own car, settled them in the back seat. He promised he would have them both safely home before the evening meal as he slid in beside Kylie who was already behind the wheel.

"Where to?" she asked flippantly.

"Avalon. Just beyond the TV studios."

Kylie turned the car away from the direction they should have been going, saying not one word about Aunt Tabitha's birthday. Once off the hill, she turned the car south along Highway 2.

"What's this with the brooch?" she asked quietly so her voice did not reach the two in the back seat.

Steven hesitated, said, "Stolen from Ancell's safe Monday night."

"Clever!" Kylie drawled, making two long syllables of the word. "How do you do it?"

"Instinct," said Steven casually. He thought about his comment to Jonas about Tai Bennett—the right man at the right time. The random factor—the chance encounter—made all the difference sometimes.

Today he had happened to be in the right place at the right time. Thanks to Aunt Tabitha. If it had not been for that venerable lady, he would have stayed home to catch up on some of the odd jobs that always seemed to accumulate behind his back. Even then, if they had left home earlier—or later—if he had not stopped to talk to Lance—

They crossed the river to Avalon, Steven directing Kylie to street and number. When they finally stopped, he sat for a moment gazing at the house where Rob Henshawe lived with his mother.

A ranch-type house built in creamy Huntly brick, windows open, suggesting someone was home. As Steven climbed out of the car, he could hear a cricket commentary coming from somewhere at the back.

He opened the door for Cliff. "Look, son, only you and I are going in there. Don't take any notice of what I say. But when I ask you a direct question, you answer yes or no. Understand?"

Cliff nodded, walked beside Steven along the drive leading to the garage at the rear of the long section. Before they reached the back of the house, a small dog bounced on to the concrete, teeth bared, growling deep in his throat, daring them to proceed.

Rob Henshawe came to their rescue, catching the dog affectionately by the scruff of his neck. "Hold on, Rascal. They're friends."

He looked curiously at Cliff lagging behind Steven. "Come on in. Getting tired of my own company anyway. Especially as we're losing." He switched off the small transistor sitting on the garden table, waited inquiringly.

Steven was relieved to learn that Mrs Henshawe was not at home.

He said quietly, "Police business, I'm afraid. We've just picked up this youngster with a stolen car. Claims you'll be able to identify him."

Rob looked at Cliff, frowned. "Well, he does look familiar. Vaguely. Am I supposed to know him?"

Steven turned to Cliff. "Is this the man you know as Chuck?"

As Cliff nodded, Rob started, looked again. "Why, you're Mrs Bullen's lad, aren't you? What are you doing down here?"

Cliff shrugged uncomfortably, began to take an interest in the dog who was sniffing at his down-held hand.

"Yes," said Steven easily. "Cliff Bullen's the name he gave. But there's also a matter of a brooch we found in his girl friend's possession. Says you sold it to the girl's mother, a Mrs Paterson." He brought out his handkerchief, unfolded it to show the surface of the brooch. "D'you recognise this brooch?"

Rob gave Steven a puzzled stare. "You know I sell that junk as a sideline, Steven. Maybe I did sell that particular one to this Mrs Paterson. Sold dozens like it. No way I can positively identify it. But if it gets the kid off the hook, yeh, okay, I sold it to Mrs Paterson. She'd know. To me, they all look alike. A bit of gold wire. A chip of glass."

"Not glass this time, Rob. A star sapphire. More important it's part of the loot stolen from Carter Ancell's safe Monday night."

Steven, watching Henshawe closely, saw his face stiffen, his eyes darken slightly.

Henshawe laughed. "Is this a gag, Steven? A come-on? That's a Delacourt brooch. Exactly the same as all the others."

"Not exactly," said Steven. He opened the handkerchief, turned the brooch over. "To start with, this is really a pendant. See this and this? That's the release for the central pendant piece—so. And that's where it clips on a gold chain to be worn around the neck. No Delacourt brooch has those. And the faulty catch. That's why it was left with Ancell. To have the catch fixed. He put it in a Delacourt box for safekeeping. Monday night you stole it. We can prove all this, Rob. Mrs Paterson will say you sold her the brooch. The owner will say she gave it to Ancell on Monday."

Rob sat down on the edge of the patio, watching Cliff playing with Rascal, face sombre. "Anything else?" he asked at last.

Steven seemed to change the subject. "Nice little dog you've got there. What's his breed?"

"Australian Silky Terrier. Mum's dog but—"

Steven nodded. "There were dog hairs on Ancell's clothing. Hairs from the coat of a Sydney Silky."

Rob was silent. He knew from experience how small pieces of evidence would be built into a case against him.

Steven sighed. "That night you turned up at the house with all that rot about Frank Summerfield and Cheapskate—you were trying to find out how much we knew, weren't you?"

"Caught on to that, did you? Can't blame a bloke for trying."

"Maybe not. But you must've known you couldn't get away with it."

"No? Cheapskate was getting away with it!"

"Two years ago Cheapskate surfaced. Hitting country areas. Towns. Cities. That was when you muscled in, wasn't it, Rob? Made Cheapskate your front. Used his methods. Drove him into the ground. The Cheapskate operating now is you. And you started three months before you left the force."

Rob hesitated, laughed. "Sure, I gave it a whirl. It was fun—and easy. If they hadn't turfed me out, I'd have dropped it. I swear, Steven." He paused. "I didn't mean to kill Ancell. Thought he'd just go into the office. But he had to come into the workshop, the damn fool. I had to do something. I mean—I was there! I couldn't let him—"

"Yeh, I know. You panicked. The way you panicked when the crowd broke that time. Lashed out. Used more force than necessary." Steven stood up. "Will you come with me now, Rob, or will I send for a car?"

"I'll come." Rob straightened. "Can I ring my mother. She's down at Nessie's. A new baby."

"Of course. What about the dog?"

"Oh, he'll be all right. I just have to say 'Stay, wait for Mumma' and he'll stick around till Mum comes back."

Steven followed him into the house, waited while he telephoned his mother to say he had been called away, waited till he locked up the house.

The last thing Rob Henshawe did was to make a farewell fuss over Rascal, the dog whose hairs would match those taken from the clothing of Carter Ancell.

If you have enjoyed this book, you might wish to join the Walker British Mystery Society.

For information, please send a postcard or letter to:

Paperback Mystery Editor

**Walker & Company
720 Fifth Avenue
New York, NY 10019**